The House
On
Ludington Street

SUSAN L. PARE'

The House on Ludington Street - All contents copyright © 2018 Susan L. Pare.

Printed in the United States of America.

First Edition: October, 2018

All rights reserved.

Cover designed by Susan L. Pare'

ISBN-13: 978-0-9966195-9-2

Table of Contents

CPSIA information can be obtained
at www.ICGtesting.com
Printed in the USA
BVOW06s0955280217
477348BV00011B/114/P

The House

On

Ludington Street

For Poop
This story might not have been written, if he hadn't been such a bad boy.

One

"Is not!"

"Is, too," John yelled back at his friend. "I know for a fact that it's there."

"How come no one knows about it, then?"

"Well, I know about it. My grandpa told me."

"Bullshit, he did. You're just making this up."

"You wanna hear the story or not?"

"Listen, Poop, I've lived here all my live. So, if it's there, how come I never heard about it until now?" Whitey asked.

"How should I know? Maybe, people don't talk about it because it's meant to be a secret."

"Screw you. You're just pulling my leg," Whitey said, reaching for a cigarette. He lit it, took a long drag, and blew out the smoke. "Want one?" he asked John.

"No. I'm trying to cut back." John thought for a few moments. "How about I have my gramps tell you the story?"

"Yeah, right! Your gramps can't remember shit these days," Whitey said, grinning.

"He remembers about the tunnel. Don't forget, he helped build City Hall."

Whitey looked at John, thinking about what John had said. "You're right. I forgot about that," he commented.

"Damn right, you forgot. He remembers everything from back then. He has stories that would make you sleep with the lights on."

"Okay. Let's go talk to him, then, and find out

1

where all the bodies are buried," Whitey said.

"Tomorrow. But, we need to ask him in the morning. He remembers better in the morning," John uttered softly.

Samuel Hassel looked his age and then some. He was pushing ninety and he spent his days sitting in a chair, looking out a window and wishing he was dead. Samuel had lived a hard life, most of it working construction. He had been implemental in building some of the more majestic structures in Columbus, such as the Tremont Hotel and City Hall. He had buried three wives, his oldest son, Samuel, Jr., and a grand-daughter.

Samuel had been living with his grandson, Isaac and Isaac's family for the past ten years. These days, it seemed the only joy in his life was when his great-grandson, John, would come into his room and visit with him.

So, last night when John mentioned that his friend, Whitey, was coming over in the morning to see him, the old man was thrilled. Teenagers, dumb as they might be, were still company and old Samuel didn't get much company these days.

He turned in his chair and grinned. "I wondered when you were gonna get here," he commented to Whitey. He looked the boy up and down and shook his head. "I swear your hair just keeps getting whiter. How you doing, boy?"

"I'm good, Mr. H. But, you're looking as old as shit," he joked. "How old are you now? A thousand?"

"Watch your mouth, boy, or I'll take my cane to your ass."

"That's enough, you two," John said.

"You wanna get me some coffee, John?" the old man asked. "And, tell your mother to keep it coming."

"She's bringing it now. Do you feel like talking this morning?"

"I always feel like talking. The problem is, no one ever feels like listening." He looked up at his great-grandson and smiled. "Just what is it you boys want to know?"

"Do you remember when you told me about the tunnel that runs under James Street?" John asked him. "You know, from City Hall to under the Soldier Memorial."

"Of course, I remember. I remember everything."

"Well, Whitey doesn't believe me, so can you tell him it's true?"

"Is that what this is all about?" Samuel asked. "That's not much of a story. At one time, there were a whole bunch of tunnels in this town. Everyone knows about the one by the Kurth Brewery. That one is still there, I believe. Some of the stores had tunnels - short tunnels, actually - going from one building to the next. Hell, I don't know why the fools didn't just build doors to get from one basement to the other."

"But, what about the one under James Street?" John asked him.

"There was a rumor about a house on Ludington Street that had a pretty long tunnel," Samuel continued, ignoring John's question. "It was almost a block long and came out across from the depot. That's where the lumber company is now. Rumor was that the wife's lovers used it to come and go without being seen, but that was just a made up story."

"Here's your coffee, Grandpa," John's mother, interrupted. She set a tray down on a small table next to Samuel and smiled. "Can I get you anything else?" she asked the old man.

"Are you still gonna make those brownies?" he asked her.

"I am. And, I'll bring you some as soon as they're ready."

"Do we have any pop?" John asked.

"We do, but you boys can't have any until later. You know it's not healthy to drink that stuff in the morning. I brought you milk. Drink that."

"I don't think that's true," John said, grinning, as he glanced over at Whitey.

"True or not, you're not having pop now," she told him. "Whitey, have some milk," she said, as she handed him the glass.

"Thank you, Mrs. H," Whitey said.

"Will you be here for dinner?" Mrs. Hassel asked Whitey.

Whitey looked questioningly at John.

"I think so, Mom," John answered.

"All right, then. I'll set an extra plate," she said, as she left the room.

"If it was there, it's probably been filled in," Samuel said, quietly. He turned and looked out of his window. "It's too bad they didn't tear that damn house down, too."

John waited. "Gramps? What are you talking

4

about?" John asked.

"Sorry. You're not in a hurry are you, Whitey?" Samuel asked.

Whitey glanced over at his friend, a questioning look on his face. John shrugged, not knowing why the old man was asking.

"Not really," Whitey told him.

"Good, because this might take a little while. So, how about I tell you about that house on Ludington Street and the family that lived there back in the early 1900's?"

"Are you talking about the house where the Pearys live?" Whitey asked him.

"That's the one. Have you boys ever been in that house?"

"No," John and Whitey said in unison.

"It's a beautiful house. You should try to see the inside sometime. Don't you go to school with one of the Peary kids? Maybe you could have him show you the house."

"Yeah, we do and it's a girl. Sarah Peary. But, I just want you to tell Whitey about the tunnel under City Hall," John said.

The old man grinned. "Exactly. Well, years ago, it used to be the Von Schmidt's house. Wilbur and Elise Von Schmidt had that house built."

"Did you help build it?" Whitey asked, looking at John, who was rolling his eyes, wondering why Samuel was talking about the house.

"Yep, I sure did. It was in 1906. I was thirty-nine years old at the time. Von Schmidt was a real bastard to work for. Nothing was ever right. It took months

5

longer to finish that place than it should have. It turned out pretty damn nice, though." Samuel took a sip of his coffee and was quiet for a few moments. "I probably worked on most of the houses that were built in this town back then," he finally continued. "Then, old Artie got me and I couldn't climb ladders anymore, so I retired."

Whitey looked at him, confused by his comment. "Artie got you? Artie who?" he asked the old man.

John laughed. "Arthritis, you dickhead. That's what Gramps calls his arthritis."

Whitey's face turned red, embarrassed at being laughed at. "Yeah, well, you're. . ." He looked away, not finishing his thought.

"Go on, Gramps," John said, patiently. "What about that house?"

T_{wo}

"You see, Wilbur Von Schmidt moved here from Chicago because he had been offered a job running the police department. Back in the early 1900s, that was a big deal. The job paid well enough, but Von Schmidt didn't take the job for the money. He was wealthy enough. I heard once that he was so well off he didn't need to work if he didn't want to. Nope he took it because Von Schmidt wanted. . . he needed to be in charge. Columbus was a growing town, and he figured he could bring in his own guys and make up his own rules. And, he did. He was one mean son of a bitch."

"Gramps, what does this have to do with the tunnel?" John asked.

Samuel grinned. "You young whippersnappers are always so impatient. Just sit back and listen and you'll find out what. Okay?"

John smiled back at him. "Okay. I'll be quiet."

The brand new 1906 Model K Ford stopped in front of the massive house. Wilbur Von Schmidt shut the engine off and turned to look at his children sitting in the back of the car.

"It's beautiful," his wife, Elsie, uttered.

"It is," Wilbur agreed. "Now, children, I have some instructions for you before you enter your new home. You will always enter through the side door or kitchen door. The front door is for guests only. You will use the back staircase to go to your room, which is on the third floor. We will be renting out the bedrooms on the second floor, so, you are to remain quiet when you are in the

7

attic. *I don't want you to disturb our renters. Is that clear?"*

"Yes, father," the three children in the back of the car muttered.

"All right, Mother," he said. *"You may take the children inside. Allow them to look around before you show them to their room."*

"Aren't you coming in?" Elise asked her husband.

"Later. I'm going over to the police station and check it out. I may be late, so feed the children early and allow them to read for a while in the sitting room before retiring to bed."

"When does Petra start?" Elise asked her husband.

"She is already here. I assigned her the back bedroom."

"Who's Petra?" Carl asked, interrupting his parent's conversation.

Wilbur brought his hand back, intending to strike the child. He hesitated, as the boy flinched. "Next time you interrupt it will be the belt. Understand?"

"Yes, Father. I'm sorry," Carl whimpered.

"Now, all of you, get out of the car. I have things to do."

Samuel took a sip of coffee and made a face. "I hate cold coffee," he said. He took another sip and set the cup down. "Like I said, Von Schmidt was a mean man. In less than a month, he had fired the three existing policemen and had hired three of his Chicago buddies. You have to remember that things were a lot different back then. A cop didn't have any formal training. Most of them were just normal guys, who wanted to earn a decent living and only shot a gun when they went hunting. But, Van Schmidt and his guys. . . well, they wanted power and money and they didn't care what they had to do to get it." He gave a small disdainful laugh. "You got to hand it to him. Every business was paying him for protection. And, the funny thing is, they were paying for that protection to the cops so they could be protected from those same cops. If you didn't go along, your windows would be broken, or worse. A couple of shop keepers had their buildings set on fire."

"How big was Columbus back then?" John asked.

"Hmm." Samuel said, thinking about the question. "I'd say around two thousand people or so. Perhaps a few more."

"So, in fifty years it's only grown by a thousand people," Whitey declared. "That doesn't seem like a lot to me."

"It isn't," Samuel agreed. "Anyway, a few years went by and by 1908 Von Schmidt had complete control of the town. Crime hardly existed and the idiots that were foolish enough to try to break the law were severely punished. I remember that he actually hung a young man for stealing a bunch of bananas from a grocery store. Bananas hadn't been sold that long in America, and, at the time, they were pretty expensive to buy. The owner decided he didn't want to press charges, but Von Schmidt said the town needed to know that no crime, no matter how big or small, would go unpunished."

"By now, Wilbur's three children were teen-agers. His son, Carl, had a job cleaning city hall after school and on Saturdays. Word on the street was that Carl and his two sisters still shared a room in the attic. That attic was cold as ice in the winter and as hot as hell in the summer. Those poor kids had to have been totally miserable."

"The three vacant upstairs' bedrooms had been rented to a couple of teachers and a stone mason. That's a brick layer, in case you didn't know that already."

"I knew that," Whitey informed him.

"Good for you," Samuel said. "Now all three of these men were single, of course. Well, Petra started to gain a lot of weight and before long it was obvious that she was pregnant. When Von Schmidt confronted her, she said that she had been raped, but wouldn't tell him which man had done the deed. Von Schmidt sat those three men down and put the fear of God in them.

"*Either you tell me which one of you did this or I'll have all three of you castrated,*" *Von Schmidt yelled. Dead silence. He stood up and pushed his chair back, towering over the men.* "*Petra,*" *he yelled.* "*Get in here.*"

Petra, her head hung low, entered the kitchen and hesitated. "*You wanted to see me?*" *she asked.*

"*Which one?*" *Von Schmidt hollowed at her.* "*You tell me or I'll shoot all three of them.*"

"*I don't know, Sir. It was dark and it was only the one time,*" *she told him, tears running down her cheeks.* "*I'm sorry, Sir. May I leave now?*"

10

"No!" Von Schmidt yelled. "You may not leave."

He pulled his .45 out of its holster and laid it on the table in front of him. "This is what is going to happen. I'm going to line you three up and every time one of you says 'it wasn't me' I'm going to shoot off one of your knee caps."

He waited a few moments. Then, in a voice as quiet as a whisper, Von Schmidt asked, "Mr. Flannagan, did you rape Petra?"

Flannagan shook his head no. "I'm sorry, Mr. Von Schmidt, but I cannot confess to something I did not do. I have no knowledge of who committed this horrible crime, but it was not I."

Von Schmidt reached for the gun, aimed it at the terrified school teacher's knee, and just as he was about to pull the trigger, the stone mason yelled. "It was me. For God's sake, don't shoot him."

Von Schmidt turned the gun away from Flannagan and pointed it at the mason. "You did this? You violated this woman? You confess that it was you?"

"I'm so sorry. But, I didn't rape her. She wanted it. She consented to it every time."

"No!" Petra cried out. "He's lying."

Samuel looked towards his bedroom door and sniffed. "Do I smell brownies?"

"Who cares about brownies?" John exclaimed. "What happened next?"

"He shot the man right between his eyes."

"Whoa!" John cried out. "Right there, in his own house?"

"Right there in the kitchen." Samuel answered,

11

trying not to smile at John's reaction. "Anyway, he sent Petra packing. I heard he gave her train fare, but who knows for sure."

"Was the train station here back then?" John inquired.

"It was. It was built the same year as that house." He looked at his watch. "Almost time for dinner and some of those brownies. Should I stop now?"

"No!" both boys yelled.

"What happened next?" Whitey asked.

"Well, not long after that, a crew of construction workers came to town. By now, Von Schmidt had asked the two teachers who had been renting bedrooms to find other living arrangements. He put the men up in his house. Mrs. Von Schmidt was working her fingers to the bone, not having a maid and all, and she complained to her husband that she had had enough and wanted him to find her help. Von Schmidt's answer to her plea was to take his two teenage daughters out of school and put them to work helping their mother in the house."

"Every day for the next two months, some of the men worked in the basement of City Hall and some worked in Von Schmidt's basement. Then, all of a sudden, one day they were gone."

"Now, I can't prove it, understand, but I think. . . Well, let's just say that might have been when the tunnel under James Street was dug out." Samuel sat back in his chair and stared at the two boys.

"Then, there is a tunnel," Whitey said.

"I'm pretty sure that's when the tunnel at that

house was dug out, too. I never saw it, of course, but what else could those men have been doing in that basement?"

"Now, the renters are gone, the construction crew is gone, and all the upstairs' bedrooms are empty. Von Schmidt finally gives in and allows his two daughters and his son to occupy two of the bedrooms. The girls go back to school and everybody's happy. Or, are they?"

The old man paused for a moment. "No. Von Schmidt can't stand the fact that he has two empty bedrooms. There's no money to be made leaving those rooms empty, so he rents them out again. This upsets his wife, Elise, who has had a break from all the extra work, and she begins to nag him."

"Who'd he rent the rooms to?" Whitey interrupted.

"A young married couple and a man who worked for the railroad. The young couple didn't last long. Von Schmidt informed them that their noisy encounters in the bedroom would not be tolerated and they were gone within a few weeks."

"Now the railroad man. . . the stationmaster, as he was called. . . was a very enjoyable gentleman. He enjoyed a glass of beer and I occasionally ran into him while I was doing the same in a local pub. He was always ready to have a conversation and most people in town liked him. He was extremely good looking, if I do say so myself. Not pretty, like some men, but rugged good looking. Most of the single women in town held high hopes that he might notice them, but he never seemed to be too interested in any of them."

"Gramps?" John quietly said.

"What?"

"How come Von Schmidt wasn't arrested after he killed the brick layer?"

"Uh huh. You picked up on that, did you? Like I said, he was the law. It was a different time, John. He pretty much did what he wanted. Today, he would have been behind bars so fast your head would spin. But, back then? Well, the body was buried and that was that."

"Doesn't seem right, somehow," Whitey commented.

"You're right. It wasn't. Now, I think I'm ready to take a break. Let's see what your mom has made for dinner."

"Just a little longer," John begged.

"After we eat."

Three

"Are you sure you don't want another helping?" Julia Hassel asked Whitey.

Whitey placed his hands on his stomach and smiled. "I'd love some more, but there's no room to put it. That was really good."

"Well, thank you, Whitey. See, John, what nice manners Whitey has."

John looked at her and burped. "Sorry. Excuse me," he said grinning. "See, I've got manners, too."

Julia shook her head, trying to hold back a smile. "You're excused." She looked over at Samuel. "Did you have enough, Grandpa?"

"I'm full." He pushed his chair away from the table and stood up. "It's time for a nap."

John's head snapped up and he looked at the old man. "It's time for what?" he asked loudly.

"My nap."

"What about the story?"

"It will keep. Right now, I'm tired and I'm going to go lie down for a while."

The boys watched as Samuel left the kitchen, their disappointment showing on their faces. "Mom?"

"You know he always naps after dinner, John. You might as well forget about the rest of the day. Anyway, you need to cut the grass."

"Ah, Mom, I just cut it a couple of days ago."

"That was a week ago. Now, out, you two. I've got dishes to wash. Unless, of course, you want to do that before you cut the grass."

The two boys jumped up off their chairs and

headed for the back door. "Thanks, Mrs. H," Whitey called over his shoulder, as he ran out the door.

"You two behave yourselves," she called out.

"Yes, ma'am. We always do," Whitey yelled back.

John finished cutting the lawn, and dropped down on the grass alongside of his friend. "Now what are we gonna do for the rest of the day?"

"We could ride out to the park and see what's happening there," Whitey replied.

"My bike has a flat," John told him.

"Well, then, let's fix it."

They turned, as they heard the back screen door slam shut. "Grandpa is awake. He wants to know if you want to come in." Julia yelled.

"Hell, yes," Whitey yelled.

"Tell him we'll be right there," John shouted.

"So, where was I?" Samuel mused, looking out of the window.

"You were telling us about the new renter. That good looking guy. Remember?" John told him.

"Ahh, that's right. Albert Borden was his name. Like I said, he was a friendly guy and well liked in town. Well, things seemed to go smoothly at the Von Schmidt house for about. . ." He hesitated, thinking. "Probably six to eight months and, then, the crap hit the fan."

"What happened?" John asked.

"The way I heard it, Von Schmidt came home, expecting his supper to be on the table as usual, and his wife was nowhere to be found. I still don't know if

16

he was more upset over the inconvenience of his supper not being ready or the fact that his wife was missing. Von Schmidt was in charge of investigating his wife's disappearance, of course, which was a joke. The man went through the motions, but after a few days he dropped the whole thing. By the time a month had passed, most people had forgotten about the whole thing and life went on as usual."

"Carl Von Schmidt, who was now working at the local newspaper, had been overheard telling a co-worker that his parents had had a horrible fight the week before his mother went missing. The following day he arrived at work with a black eye and numerous cuts and bruises on his face. Two days later, he was seen, carrying a couple of suitcases, boarding the train to Chicago. That was the last anyone saw of him."

"Von Schmidt's two daughters were now caring for the house, doing the cooking and cleaning. Of course, with only their father and Borden there, it was a lot easier for them than it had been. . . Vivian and Beth!" he suddenly exclaimed, making Whitey jump.

"Their names were Vivian and Beth. Damn! I finally remembered. I've been trying to remember those girls' names for hours." He grinned. "Some things may take a little longer these days, but I still manage to get there. Anyway, it was a lot easier for them than it had been for their mother. How about something to drink?"

John stared at him. "What?"

"I need something to drink. Go see if there's any beer in the frig."

"You know mom doesn't want you drinking beer," John declared.

"If she sees you, make it a Coke. Otherwise, bring me a beer."

"All right. Whitey, do you want anything?" John asked, as he started towards the door.

"I'll have a Coke, too," Whitey answered. "Lots of ice."

"Me, too," Samuel added. "Lots of ice, if it's a Coke. But, no ice for the beer," he said, laughing.

John smiled as he left the room. "Be right back," he said.

"I'll be right back, too," Samuel told Whitey. "I've got to pee."

"Now, I'm gonna try to get the rest of the story in order, but I may be a little off, so bear with me. There were three important things that happened in Columbus in the matter of a few months. If I recall correctly, it was 1921. Von Schmidt had been running the town for fifteen years."

"His daughters, now grown women, were both teachers and still lived at home. They were strange women – both of them. They only left the house during the week to go to work. They'd come home, fix supper, and retire to their rooms. They kept up the house, cleaning and washing clothes on week-ends." Samuel thought for a moment. "Now that I think of it, I never saw those women up close. I couldn't tell you if they were pretty or ugly, fat or thin. They lived in this town for years and no one really knew them."

He took a swallow of his beer and burped. "Well, Von Schmidt didn't know it, but he was about to get his comeuppance. Some of the merchants in town had finally had enough and decided Von Schmidt had to go. A bunch of them met with the FBI in Madison and asked for their help."

"The Bureau hadn't been around that long, and prohibition had just started. The FBI told the merchants that they would look into it and that they would send an agent to check it out as soon as one was available. Well, weeks went by, and nothing changed. The merchants figured they were on their own. Peter Polsen, who ran the local hardware store, started holding secret meetings with some of the other merchants to plan an attack on the police department."

"What? No way!" Whitey said, laughing. "That never happened."

"I didn't say it did. The attack may not have happened, but the meetings and the planning did. Everyone was sitting in Polsen's kitchen, just two nights away from executing their plan, when the door swung open and a giant walked in."

"A giant, Gramps?" John asked.

"Yes, a giant. You do know that the further back you go in time, the shorter the men were. You were taught that in school, weren't you?"

"No, I don't remember being taught that. How about you, Whitey? Do you remember being taught that?"

"I must have been sick that day. Sorry, Mr. H. I didn't mean to laugh. Just how big was this giant?"

"Make fun if you want, but I met Agent Alexander Harman and that man was at least six feet seven inches. That's tall, even by today's standards, don't you think?"

"I guess," John replied.

"Well, back then he was a giant. Anyways, he had been in town watching Von Schmidt. He had heard about the attack and decided it was time to step in."

The door swung open and FBI agent Harman stepped into the kitchen. The men sitting at the table jumped up, ready to do battle with the intruder.

"Take it easy," Harman said. "I'm with the FBI and you are about to make the biggest mistake of your lives."

"Show us your ID."

Harman pulled his ID wallet out of his breast pocket and flashed his badge. "Satisfied?" he asked.

"What are you doing here?" Polsen asked. "And, what do you mean that we're going to make the biggest mistake of our lives?"

"I've been in town every night since you met with the agents in Madison. I'm tracking Von Schmidt, and he's about to be arrested, so I'm asking you all to stay out of this. We've got enough on him right now to put him away for years."

Polsen sat back in his chair and gave a sigh of relief. "Thank god. I have seriously been thinking of moving my family to another town. The atrocities that have been committed by that man and his goons are unbelievable. We can't make a decent living, with his hands in our pockets. We're tired of paying him off so we can stay in business," he said, raising his voice. "My god, he actually hung a young man for stealing some bananas?"

"Hell, he shot that boarder right between the eyes, in his own kitchen," Melvin Kraute added.

"And, no one really knows what happened to his wife. She could be buried in the back yard for all we know," Paul Linquest chimed in.

"These situations are all going to be addressed. I'm just asking that you don't do or say anything foolish. We need a few more days to lock it up. We've got a case, all right. But, in a few more days we'll have an air tight case." Harman glanced towards the kitchen sink. "Would you mind if I get a glass of water?" he asked Polsen.

"Help yourself," Polsen replied.

"We'll hold off for a few more days," Kraute told Harman. "But, if something isn't done pretty damn soon, we're going through with this."

"Trust me," Harman said. "It's in the works. Von Schmidt is going down."

"You damn right he's going down," Linquest muttered. "One way or the other."

"Mr. H?" Whitey interrupted

"Yes, Whitey."

"How do you know all this? About what was said and stuff."

Samuel paused for a moment. "I remember it because I was there."

"What?" John exclaimed. "No way."

Samuel grinned. "Yes. Way."

"Wow," Whitey said, grinning. "You were one tough dude, weren't you?"

"I had my moments." Samuel said. He looked away and sighed. "I'm sorry, boys, but I've had enough for one day. How about we pick this up some other time?" Samuel asked.

"When? Tomorrow?" John asked.

"That's fine. Or, the next day," Samuel told him.

"I'll check with him tomorrow morning and give you a call," John told Whitey. "He's always more alert in the morning."

"I can hear you, you know," the old man said.

"I know, Gramps."

F_{our}

"Don't you have a baseball game this morning?" Isaac Hassel asked his son.

"Raining."

Isaac looked out the window and frowned. "Not here, it isn't."

"Whitey said it's raining at the park."

"So, you're going to let the team down and not show up?" his father asked him.

"Game's been cancelled."

John's father sat down at the kitchen table and looked at his son. "Can you tell me why the game has been cancelled? You know it's not raining outside, don't you?"

"Whitey said a lot of the guys are sick."

"Really?" Isaac asked.

"Yep. Must be something going around."

"Is Whitey sick?" his father asked.

"I don't think so. He sounded okay on the phone."

"Well, if you're not going to your game, what are you planning on doing today?"

John finished off his cereal and stood up. "Well, seeing as how it's probably gonna rain, we thought we'd visit with Gramps this morning."

"Really? It seems like you're spending a lot of time with him."

"He's a pretty interesting guy, Dad."

"Really? I'm glad you think so. When is Whitey coming over?"

"He's on his way."

23

Samuel smiled as the two boys sat down on the floor in front of him. He finished off his cup of coffee and cleared his throat. "It's now 1921. Prohibition was a big deal and law enforcement – especially the FBI - wasn't big enough to catch all the bad guys. Moonshine was a big money maker and we had a lot of it going on right around here. The big cities, like Milwaukee and Chicago were like war zones, with the feds fighting the gangs and the gangs fighting each other."

"Von Schmidt had a small crew hijacking trucks and stealing the liquor. He didn't do it very often, so he stayed under the radar and the general consensus was that Capone or one of his rivals had done it. The hijackers would drive the truck to Columbus, unload it, and ditch it a hundred miles or more away from town. No one ever put two and two together and figured it out. Until Agent Harman started watching Von Schmidt, that is."

"Now here's where the story gets good. The trucks would pull up and park across from the railroad station, where a couple of Von Schmidt's goons would be waiting. They'd unload the truck and within minutes the truck was gone. Then, it was just a matter of carrying the booze through the tunnel into the basement of Von Schmidt's house."

"A few days after Agent Harman had talked to us at Polsen's house, Von Schmidt's house was raided by the feds. His basement was packed with hundreds of cases of booze. He had never sold a bottle of the stuff that he had stolen. He figured he had plenty of time and if he waited until the supply was really low and the demand high, he'd get top dollar for it."

"The feds asked a couple of cops from Madison to take over the police department until a new force could be hired. Von Schmidt's men were held in jail while all the charges could be sorted out." Samuel paused for a few moments. "This is where it went wrong," he continued. "They placed Von Schmidt under house arrest. They actually allowed him to stay in his house, rather than putting him behind bars with his cronies."

"I don't know what the feds were thinking. They assigned one cop to watch him twenty-four seven. He stayed in the house with Von Schmidt, his two daughters and the boarder, Albert Borden. For god's sake, the man couldn't stay awake forever."

"Two days! Can you believe that? Two days before anyone checked on the cop. Of course, he was dead. Shot right between the eyes, just like that poor stone mason had been years ago. Von Schmidt's two daughters were found in the basement, tied up and gagged, laying in their own piss and shit."

"Gross," Whitey cried out. "That's really gross."

"Yeah? Well, how do you think the two women felt? The youngest one, Beth, spent the next six months in a mental hospital, trying to get over the trauma she'd gone through. Vivian, though. . . Well, Vivian talked. Once she started there was no stopping her. The things that those children endured in that house were horrifying. Carl, especially, was beaten regularly from the time he was just a little boy until he finally got the nerve to walk away. Although, the girls weren't sexually molested, their father forced them to

25

watch him having sex with their mother. And, from what Vivian told the feds, it was rough sex – mean sex, with whips and that kind of shit."

"Wow!" John said. "People do that stuff?"

"Some like it rough," Samuel replied. "Although, Vivian did say that her mother was an unwilling partner. Now, Albert Borden is a different story. He lived in that house with Von Schmidt for over ten years. According to Vivian, they started sleeping together a few months after her mother left."

"Vivian and Borden slept together?" John asked.

Samuel laughed. "No. Borden and Von Schmidt were lovers.

"No way!" Whitey shouted. "That's so gross."

"That type of life style was totally frowned upon back then. No one ever came out of the closet like you see happening today. But, I guess whenever or wherever, it's always gone on. Anyway, Von Schmidt and Borden disappeared and no one had a clue where they had gone. Vivian kept up the house until her sister was released from the hospital. They eventually sold the house and moved. I heard they went to live with their brother, who was working in Milwaukee. But, who knows for sure."

"Did the cops ever find Von Schmidt?" John asked.

"Oh, yeah. They found him and Borden a few weeks after they disappeared. They were in Von Schmidt's car, which had been parked in a corn field off of an old county road. It looked like they'd been dead for about a week or so. The feds ruled it a suicide/murder thing and that was that. The town hired some new cops, who did a pretty decent job and eventually everything got back to normal."

Whitey looked up at the old man.

"What?" Samuel asked him.

"You lived here all the time this was going on, didn't you? It must have been horrible."

"It was what it was. I made a living, took care of my family, and minded my own business."

"So, that's it?" John asked, looking disappointed. "What about the tunnel at city hall? Is there one there or not?"

Five

"You boys want a break?" Samuel asked.

"No, thanks," John told him.

"I don't want a break. I want to know if there's a tunnel there or not," Whitey replied.

Samuel stood up and stretched. "Well, I need to pee. I'll be back in a minute, so if you want anything to drink you better get it now."

Whitey watched the old man leave the room. "Hey, Poop. I could go for a Coke. Will you get me one?"

"What am I – your slave? Go get it yourself and bring me one, too."

"So, that makes me your slave," Whitey said, laughing. He stood up and headed for the bedroom door. "Do you think he's ever going to tell us about the tunnel?" he asked his friend.

John shook his head. "Damned if I know, but it's kinda cool listening to him, isn't it?"

"If you remember, I mentioned that the Von Schmidt sisters sold the house and moved to Milwaukee. After. . ."

"I remember that," Whitey replied.

"Yeah, me, too," John said.

The old man looked at them and smiled. "Good. I'm glad you were paying attention. Anyway, what I didn't tell you was who bought the house. It took a while to sell it, of course, with everything that had happened there. There were lots of lookers, but those were mostly people who were curious to see where the murders had taken place and weren't really interested in buying it."

"It was probably seven or eight months later, when the circus came to town. Circuses weren't much back then. Just a big tent with a few elephants that did some tricks, some trapeze artists, and a bunch of clowns that acted stupid. But, it was a change from the everyday humdrum and most of the town would show up. However, it was the games that most people enjoyed. Shoot the ducks and win a prize. Knock over the bottles and take home a fish. That kind of stuff. A favorite was the fortune teller. For a dime, this woman, who wore a pound of makeup, would tell you your future."

"Did you ever have you fortune told, Gramps?" John asked him.

"I did."

"Did it come true?"

"It did."

"What did she tell you?" Whitey asked.

"That I would marry often and live a long life."

"How often?" Whitey asked.

"Gramps was married three times," John said, grinning. "He was so hard to live with, they all died to get away from him. Right, Gramps?"

"Unfortunately, that's pretty close to the truth. But, I loved them all, even if it was for a short time."

"I'm never getting married," Whitey declared.

"I'll bet you anything you'll be married before John here," Samuel said, grinning. "Should I continue with my story?"

"Yes, please," John said.

"The fortune teller's name was Agatha Birdsey. I'll never forget it. The kids called her Birdseed. Well, she and the sword swallower from the circus decided to buy the house, made an offer, it was accepted, and that was that. We never did find out if she was married to that man or not. You may never meet carnies or circus people, but you can believe me when I tell you they are a strange lot. The first thing they did was completely redecorate the inside. They hung heavy velvet curtains in all the downstairs windows, making it so dark inside that you needed to turn the lights on during the day in order to see. She advertised that she was open for business by hanging a big sign in the front window. To this day, I will never understand how that woman thought she could make a living, in this town, telling fortunes."

"Suddenly, there were stories around town about a ghost living in the house. And, it was a mean ghost. Mirrors would suddenly shatter, vases would be knocked over, the lights flickered on and off. . ." Samuel hesitated. "I'm trying to remember exactly. . ." He smiled. "Yes. That's it. The police got a phone call from Agatha saying that her friend had been stabbed and she needed help. When they arrived at the house, Franco – that was the name of the sword swallower - was on the floor with a sword sticking out of his chest. 'It was the ghost! The ghost stabbed my Franco,' Agatha kept yelling. They rushed Franco to the hospital, where he died without ever saying a word."

"It was one of his swords," she said, sobbing. "He always kept them in the room at the top of the

stairs. *He had been up there practicing his sword swallowing and I heard him call out. The next thing I knew, he had tumbled down the steps. I ran to help him, and he was just lying there. There was blood everywhere. I asked him what had happened and he whispered that it was the ghost. The ghost grabbed one of his swords and plunged it into his chest."*

Police Chief Hazelman looked down at the body, thinking that he must have taken quite a bit of strength to ram that sword through the man's body. 'How much strength does a ghost have?' he caught himself wondering. He shook the stupid thought from his mind, and turned to Agatha. "Was there anyone else in the house when this happened?"

"No, just my Franco and me. And, that horrible ghost."

"Ma'am, you know there's no such thing as ghosts, don't you?" Hazelman asked her.

She looked at him, her mouth hanging open in shock. "No ghosts? You don't think there are ghosts? Then, you tell me, hey! Who turns the lights on and off? Who breaks things and throws things across the room? Not me and not my poor Franco. It's the ghost. A woman ghost, she is."

"Do you think it's possible that he tripped and impaled himself as he fell?"

"No! No! No!" Agatha yelled. "He no trip." She fell to her knees in anguish. "I need to go to my Franco now. He needs me," she shouted. She reached for her shawl, that was lying on a chair next to her.

"Sorry, Miss Birdsey, but you can't leave right now. Your friend, your husband. . . I'm sorry, but he

31

didn't make it. He's dead."

"My Franco dead? No. Tell me it's not true."

"It's true and I'm arresting you for his murder."
He looked over at a young police officer who was
watching the scenario take place. "Officer, please cuff
Miss Birdsey."

As the officer started to walk towards Agatha, the
doorbell rang. He glanced at the police chief. "Do you
want me to answer that?"

"That seems like the thing to do," Hazelman
replied.

Just as the young cop opened the door, the
doorbell rang again. He looked around, then, glanced
back at Hazelman. "There's no one here," he said, as
the bell rang once again.

"It's the ghost," Agatha cried out. "She's making
fun at you."

"There are no ghosts," Hazelman shouted,
ducking just in time to avoid getting hit, as a small
figurine of a young boy came flying past his head."

"Chief Hazelman stood his ground. Even after
what he had witnessed in Birdsey's house, he would
not accept her word that a ghost had killed Franco.
She stood trial a month later. She had an excellent
attorney, who put both Chief Hazelman and the young
cop on the stand. They testified to what had happened
while they were they. The verdict came back 'not guilty'
and Agatha Birdsey was a free woman."

She put the house up for sale and went back to
work at the circus telling fortunes. The house didn't
sell and it went into foreclosure. It was two years

before the bank finally found a buyer."

Whitey looked at Samuel, trying not to laugh. "A ghost?"

"Seriously, Gramps," John said. "That didn't happen."

Samuel stared at the two boys. "Hard to believe, isn't it? What if I told you that I was in that house and I saw some pretty strange things going on? Would you believe me, then?"

"When were you there?"

"I was there for the cleansing of the house. It was in 1925, right before the house was sold to the Walkers."

"What's a cleansing?" John asked.

"A priest comes in and sprinkles holy water throughout the house, says a few prayers, and tries to get rid of evil spirits."

"Why were you there?" Whitey inquired.

"Well, I was asked because I had helped build that house. They figured, if there were a few hiding places, I could show them where they were."

"Were there any?" John asked.

"Nah. Anyway, there wasn't much more talk about ghosts after that. At least, not for a while."

"Do you figure that Birdseed lady killed him? You know, the sword swallower."

"She might have, but I guess we'll never know for sure, will we?"

"I have to pee," Whitey said, standing up.

"Check to see when dinner will be ready, will you?" Samuel asked him.

"Your folks aren't here," Whitey told John, as he came back into the bedroom.

John looked at the clock on the old man's dresser and checked the time. "It's only ten-thirty. They'll be back by dinner time. Go on, Gramps. Then what happened?"

Samuel cleared his throat. "Now, it's 1925. Columbus is doing pretty good. The town is growing, more merchants are opening stores, and there are a lot more cars on the streets now than horses and buggies. Chief Hazelman took a job in Madison and is gone. Henry Walker is now the new chief of police, and the new owner of that house."

"Whaat?" Whitey said. "Another cop bought the house?"

"He did. He moved in the end of August in 1925. It was a while before we realized that there was no Mrs. Walker and that she had passed some years before. His two sons and his mother lived in that house with him."

"I talked to him a few times. He liked to have an occasional beer and I'd see him in Kurth's or one of the other taverns in town. He was a pleasant fellow, very easy to talk to. I asked him once if there were any strange things happening in his house and he just laughed. Told me he had heard all the stories, but so far the ghost hadn't visited them."

"His boys. . . What were their names?" Samuel looked towards the window, thinking. "Shit! I can't remember. Anyway, the youngest boy started his last year in school that fall. He was a smart one, he was.

34

Back then, it was unusual for boys to stay in school that long. Most dropped out after eighth grade to help work the farm or get a job. But, that boy was still in school. One time, their dad told me that he wanted him to go on to a university"

"It didn't take long before it became obvious that the oldest one was on the slow side." Samuel paused for a moment. "His name was John Henry. I always wondered why they used both of his names," he said. "Anyway, school had been pretty difficult for him and he never made it to eighth grade. John Henry was a few years older than his brother and he was a big kid. He had to weigh in at least two fifty and he was tall. I'd say he was probably six two or three. Jacob. . ." Samuel grinned. "I finally, got the other one. Jacob was just the opposite. He was, maybe, five eight at the most and skinny."

Whitey looked towards the bedroom door. "Did you hear something?"

"I think my parents are home," John replied.

"Good. I'm starving," Samuel commented. "Let's go get something to eat."

Six

Julia Hassel looked over at Whitey and smiled. "You look like you're really enjoying that sandwich, Whitey," she declared.

"You make a mean egg salad, Mrs. H," he said, grinning. "What's your secret?"

John rolled his eyes. "What? You gonna be a cook now?"

"Hey! You never know. I'm never getting married, so I guess I better learn these things."

Samuel chuckled. "He keeps saying that, but the way the girls chase him, he'll probably knock some girl up and have to get married."

"Grandpa!" Julia yelled. "That's a horrible thing to say. Whitey, don't you pay any attention to him."

"That's okay, Mrs. H. I've heard that kind of talk before."

John coughed and looked away, trying not to laugh.

"Are you okay, John?" his mother asked.

"I'm fine," John said. He looked over at Samuel. "Are you planning on taking another nap today?" he asked.

"I always take a nap and today is no exception."

"Should we hang around until you wake up?" John asked the old man.

"What if I don't wake up? You'd be hanging around here forever."

"Gramps, don't say that. You're gonna wake up."

"Today, maybe. But, one of these days. . ." He looked away. "Maybe, we should skip this afternoon and pick it up tomorrow. What do you say?"

"Ahh," John said, disappointed. "But, why. . ." His mother gave him 'the look' and he didn't finish the sentence. "Okay, then, Gramps. Tomorrow, it is."

"Hey, Poop, how about we go fishing? I hear the bullheads are biting," Whitey said.

"The bullheads are always biting."

"So, do you want to?" Whitey inquired.

"Is it okay, Mom?" John asked his mother.

"Just be home in time for supper," she told him.

"How you feeling today, Mr. H?" Whitey asked.

"I'm feeling good. I got a good night's rest."

"Glad to hear it."

"How long before you boys go back to school?" Samuel asked John.

"Three weeks. We go back the day after Labor Day."

"Mr. H?"

"Yes, Whitey. What it is?"

"Is there a tunnel under City Hall or not?"

Samuel looked down at him and frowned. "Are you getting tired of my stories, Whitey?"

"Oh, no," Whitey exclaimed. "I could listen to your stories all day, but I'm just wondering if there really is a tunnel there, that's all."

"I'll make a deal with you," Samuel said. "If you don't ask me that damn question again, I'll tell you if there's one there or not. But, when I get good and ready. Okay?"

Whitey thought for a moment. "Okay. It's a deal."

"Good. Now where did I leave off yesterday?"

"You were just starting to tell us about the Walkers."

"Right," Samuel agreed. "Let's see, now." He thought for a moment. "John Henry. I was talking about him. Like I said, he was slow. His grandmother pretty much watched him during the day, gave him jobs to do around the house and such. Sometimes, his father would take him to work with him, and he would sweep out the rooms and empty the trash. And, sometimes, John Henry would disappear and be gone for hours at a time. No one ever found out where he went and no amount of questioning could get him to tell."

"About six months after they moved here, a young girl went missing. Her name was Emmy Mae Mason. She was sixteen years old and a very pretty young thing. She had a part time job working for Mrs. Hewitt after school, helping her make and repair toys."

"What?" John said. "They had stores for that?"

"I imagine they did in some towns. Here though, Mrs. Hewitt worked out of her house. Kids didn't have a lot of toys back then. The good ones cost a lot of money and if they broke, and they could afford it, they would have them repaired. Dolls were usually made one at a time and required a good deal of work and detail. But, mostly, toys were made to last. I'd say the biggest repair jobs were replacing eyes on dolls and noses on teddy bears. But, whatever it was, Mrs. Hewitt could fix the problem. Emmy Mae was a good worker, always showing up on time and never missing work."

38

"So, one day when Emmy Mae was late for work, Mrs. Hewitt was quite concerned. She did have a phone and, after waiting only an hour, she called Emmy Mae's mother. Mrs. Mason called her husband, who immediately started to trace the route that Emmy Mae took from school to Mrs. Hewitt's home. Passing an empty lot, only a few blocks from the school, he noticed movement behind some overgrown bushes. He called out 'what are you doing over there?' and saw a man run into the woods. Afraid of what he might find, he cautiously approached the area and found his daughter, shaken up but still alive."

"Did they catch the guy" Whitey asked.

"Emmy Mae said it was John Henry, but he hadn't hurt her. He was waiting outside the school and when he saw her, he pulled her behind the bushes. He told her he wanted to be her friend, and just wanted to talk to her. She started to yell but he put his hand over her mouth and told her to be quiet. When she realized he didn't mean to hurt her, she sat with him and talked. Emmy Mae kept her cool, hoping that someone would come along looking for her. Afterwards, feeling sorry for him, she asked her parents to just let it go. Chief Walker, John Henry's father, promised that nothing like that would happen again. He said he would have a long talk with John Henry and he made John Henry apologize. John Henry said he was sorry and that was it."

"It sounds like he was lonely," John said.

"It sounds like he was stupid," Whitey declared.

"He didn't really know any better. The poor boy belonged in an institution, but Walker thought that

39

between him and his grandmother they could keep him under control."

"Time passed, and the whole thing was forgotten. Until one day, a second girl didn't make it home from school. They searched the town for days, but she wasn't found. She lived a few blocks from the Walker house, so she usually passed by it on her way home. John Henry sometimes waited for her on the porch, so he could wave to her. John Henry's grandmother swore that her grandson never left the house the entire day, but everyone in town figured it was him who had taken her."

"What was her name?" John asked.

Samuel looked at him and pondered the question. "I don't remember, exactly. It will probably come to me," he finally replied. "Anyway, weeks went by. The town had been searched from one end to the other and everyone had pretty much given up trying to find her. Then, on his way to work one morning, Chief Walker noticed a bundle resting up on the fire escape on the side of City Hall. As he started to climb the stairs to retrieve the bundle, he noticed a strong odor filling the air. Well, needless to say, boys, it was that young girl rotting away in a gunny sack. It took a while to positively identify her. The cause of death couldn't be determined, due to the amount of decomposition. However, the coroner said that there was no doubt that she had been murdered."

Samuel reached for his coffee cup, started to take a sip, and put the cup back on the small table. "This is as cold as my first wife on our wedding night," he said, laughing. "John, go see if there's any coffee

40

left in the pot."

"What's a gunny sack?" Whitey asked the old man.

"It's a bag. A burlap bag. You never heard of a gunny sack before?"

"Nope," Whitey replied.

"Just what the hell do they teach you kids in school these days?" Samuel commented, shaking his head.

"Not that kind of stuff," Whitey said.

"Coffee's gone," John said, as he came back into the room.

"Just as well, I guess," Samuel said. He sat back in his chair and sighed. "Well, the town was up in arms. They were sure that John Henry had killed that girl and hid her body. The fact that his father was Chief of Police here made it all the worse. But, Chief Walker swore that his son never left the house the day that girl went missing or the night before he found her body. With no evidence to the contrary, John Henry was a free man."

"Do you think that girl would be alive today if that Emmy Mae person had pressed charges when John Henry grabbed her that day?" John asked.

"Probably not."

"Why not?" Whitey inquired.

"I'll tell you in a minute. But, I just thought of something rather interesting, that happened right around that time, that put Columbus on the map."

"What?" John inquired.

"Mrs. Maisie Power's cat had kittens."

"Whaat?" Whitey cried out. "That's no big deal.

Lots of cats have kittens."

"Not sixteen at a time, they don't," Samuel said, grinning. "At the time, it was the biggest litter of kits ever in the history of the world. People came from all over to see them. Newspapers from all over the country sent reporters and photographers to document the event. The mother cat couldn't feed them all, of course, so Mrs. Powers gave the kittens to people who could take care of them." Samuel chuckled. "If I recall correctly, she gave each of us an eyedropper when we took a kitten. It was a big deal at the time. The hotels were filled and the restaurants fed more people than ever before."

John stared at his great-grandfather, trying to figure out if the old man was serious or not. "You're kidding, right?" he finally asked. "How come I've never heard about this before?"

"You took one of the kittens?" Whitey inquired.

"Sure did. We named him Smokey Joe and he lived to be 14 years old. He was a sweet thing. It broke my heart when he passed."

"Serious? Sixteen kittens?" John said, still not sure if he should believe Samuel or not.

"Is your dad home?" Samuel asked John.

"I don't think so," John told him. "Why?"

"Well, tonight you ask him about Mrs. Power's cat. He'll tell you it really happened."

"Deal," John said, grinning. "Okay, so what happened next?"

"You mean to the cat?" Samuel asked.

"No, Gramps, not the dumb cat. What happened with John Henry?"

Samuel sat back in his chair, thinking. "I wish I had my pipe. I used to think better when I had my pipe in my hand. So, let's see. Well, about a week after that girl's body was found, John Henry and his grandmother left town. Chief Walker told everyone that his son was being evaluated by some big deal psychiatrist in Milwaukee. I have to tell you boys, the whole town breathed a little easier with that boy being out of town."

"Winter came and went and it was now the spring of 1926. Except for the normal petty stuff that every town endures, Columbus hadn't experienced any more serious crimes."

"Then, one day, Chief Walker's mother was seen shopping at a local market. No one knew she was back in town, and, everyone figured that if she was in town, it stood to reason that John Henry was also. The Mayor, upon hearing the news, immediately approached Chief Walker and inquired to the whereabouts of his son, John Henry."

"Don't you think you should have informed us that John Henry was back in Columbus?" Mayor Chadborne asked Police Chief Walker, as he ran into the police station.

Walker looked up from his desk, surprised at the outburst. "What?"

"I just heard that John Henry is back in town," the Mayor said. "Why wasn't I informed of this?"

"Well, look at you, all huffy and puffy. You better sit down, Nathaniel, before you give yourself a heart attack."

43

"I'm fine," Chadborne stated, as he leaned on the desk next to him. "I'm just fi-fine," he stuttered.

"I didn't know you stuttered," Walker declared, smiling.

Chadborne took a deep breathe. "I don't. So, what do you have to say for yourself?"

"First of all, Nathaniel, I wasn't aware that I had to inform you of my family's comings and goings. You are one of the many people in this town who accused John Henry of a crime he didn't commit. So, unless you are here to discuss city business, I have nothing to say to you."

"You know people are afraid of him," the Mayor told him. "Remember what he did to Emmy Mae. There's no denying he did that, Henry. And, we still don't know who killed Franny Franklin, do we?"

"Well, I know who didn't kill her," Walker shouted. "I know it sure as hell wasn't John Henry."

"And, I know that this town doesn't want him roaming our streets. Is that understood?" the Mayor snapped back at him.

"I'll tell you what's understood, you. . ." Hearing a noise, Walker turned and looked over at the door. Edward Jones ran into the room and stared at the Police Chief. "Are you all right," Walker asked him. "You're as white as a ghost."

"It's my girl, Chief. We can't find Emily."

"I knew something like this was going to happen," the Mayor shouted. "Where's John Henry?"

"Shut up, Nathaniel," Walker yelled. He turned to Edward Jones. "When did you last see her?"

"When she left for school this morning," Jones

replied. "Oh, my god," he cried out. "We've got to find her before it's too late."

"See now, what happened? John Henry took another girl. I'll have your badge for this," Mayor Chadborne cried out, as Jones and Walker started to run out of the room.

Walker stopped dead in his tracks, turned, and looked Chadborne straight in the eyes. "Just for your information, Nathaniel, John Henry is still in Milwaukee."

"Wow!" Whitey said. "So, who did it?"

"Franny Franklin was the name of the girl who was murdered, then?" John asked Samuel.

"That's right," Samuel replied. "Franny Franklin was the poor girl's name," he said softly. He turned away, not wanting the boys to see a tear in the corner of his eye.

"Dinner," Julia said, poking her head in the door. "Hope everyone's hungry."

Seven

"Julia?"

"Yes, Grandpa," she said.

"Do you know where my box of stuff is?" Samuel asked her.

"What stuff are you referring to? There are several boxes of yours up in the attic with old clothes in them. Plus, your chest is up there."

"That's what I want. My chest."

"What in the world do you want that old thing for?" Isaac asked. He looked at John. "Pass the potatoes, please."

"It has all my old pictures and letters in it. I believe it has some old newspaper clippings, too. I need to get something."

"You know you can't climb those stairs to the attic," Isaac declared. "Tell me what you're looking for and I'll get it for you after we're done eating."

"I want a newspaper clipping from 1926."

John's head jerked up and he stared at Samuel.

"What in the world for?" Julia asked.

"So, I can show John the article about the kittens. He doesn't believe me."

"I didn't say I didn't believe you, Gramps. I said it was really hard to believe that story."

"And, the difference is. . .?"

Isaac laughed. "You can believe him, John. There were sixteen kittens born that day. Largest litter ever, to date, as far as we know. Grandpa and grandma took one of them. I kind of remember that cat, although I was just a kid at the time." He thought for a moment, then, grinned. "Joe was his name. No, that's not it."

"Close," Samuel declared.

"I got it!" Isaac exclaimed. "Smokey Joe. That was his name. He was a real nice cat."

The old man looked at John and stuck out his tongue. "So, there. Told ya."

Whitey and John were sitting on the lawn next to the library, staring at City Hall. "I don't know if we can get up there. The fire escape is kinda high."

"Hell, Poop, why don't we just walk in through the front door?" Whitey said. "If anyone says anything, we'll tell them we need to use the john."

"Do you know which door goes up there?"

"How many doors can there be? We'll just try them all."

"We might find the door to the basement," John said. "We could look around down there and see if there's a secret entrance to the tunnel."

Whitey lay back on the lawn and looked up at the sky. "I can't believe we're gonna be seniors this year," he commented. "What are you gonna do after we graduate?"

"I don't know. I was thinking about college," John said. "But, I'll probably enlist first and get that out of the way."

"Army?" Whitey asked.

"Not for me. I'm gonna go Navy, for sure."

"I'll probably join the Army," Whitey told him. "Hey, how about we join together?"

"Fine if you want to go Navy, 'cause I'm not

joining the Army."

"You know I get seasick," Whitey reminded him.

"How well do you know Sarah Peary?" John blurted out, changing the subject.

"As well as you do, I guess. She was in a couple of my classes, but we didn't talk much," Whitey replied. "Why?"

"Do you think she'd show us through her house?"

Whitey sat straight up and grinned. "She might if we have a good reason to ask her."

"What about her folks? I heard her old man is kinda mean," John said.

"Yeah, I heard that, too. But, he's probably not home. I think he travels during the week, being a salesman and all."

"What about her mom? Is she nice?" John inquired.

"She ran off a few years ago," Whitey told him. "I think Sarah was in eighth grade when she took off. Sarah came home from school one day and her mom had packed up and left. She never even said good-bye to Sarah or her brothers and sisters."

John glanced over at his friend and shook his head. "I can't believe a mom would do that. I know my mom would never leave me."

"Mine either," Whitey said. "How about we take a walk?"

"Down Ludington Street?" John asked, grinning.

"Can't hurt." Whitey said, as he stood up and brushed off his Levi's.

"You ring the bell," John said, pushing Whitey in front of him.

"Don't push me," Whitey whispered. "What if her old man is home?"

"Then, we'll just ask him if Sarah is here."

"Why do we want to see her, anyway? What are you gonna tell him?"

"I don't know," John said.

"My dad isn't home," Sarah declared, as she came around the corner of the porch. "And, even if he was, he isn't going to bite you, you know."

John and Whitey grinned and backed away from the front door. "I didn't know you were home," Whitey told her.

"Well, I am. What do you guys want?"

John looked at Whitey. "Ask her," he said.

"You ask her," Whitey replied.

"You know you can do that all day, or one of you can tell me what you want," Sarah said, smiling. "Come on. Out with it."

"Well, my gramps has been telling us some stories about. . . Well, we were wondering if you would show us the inside of your house," John told her.

"What for?" Sarah inquired, curious about what was going on.

"Poop's grandpa told us about some stuff that went on here a long time ago, and . . . Well, he helped build this house and he thought that you might let us look around a little and. . ." Whitey looked over at John. "You tell her," he said.

"Why do you call him Poop?" Sarah asked, grinning. "That's a horrible name."

49

Whitey shrugged. "I can't remember. So, is it okay? Will you let us look around?"

"What exactly do you think you're gonna find? It's just a regular house."

"I'd like to see the basement, if that's okay," Whitey told her. "And, the attic," he added.

Sarah studied the boys, trying to determine if they were serious or playing some kind of a game. "You sure you don't want to case the joint, so you can rob us blind while we're sleeping?" she said, smiling.

John grinned. "Promise. We just want to look around."

"I guess it's okay. But, we need to use the side door."

"Why can't we go in here?" John asked, indicating the front door.

"We never use that door," Sarah told him. "We did one time and it took forever to get that ghost back outside where she belonged."

John poked Whitey in the ribs. "What the hell?" he mouthed, as Whitey grinned.

Eight

John poked his head in the bedroom, looking for Samuel. "He's not here," he told Whitey.

"I thought he was gonna tell us what happened to that girl Emily," Whitey said.

"Mom!" John yelled.

"I'm in the kitchen," she called to him. "And, stop that shouting. I'm not deaf, you know."

"Where's Gramps," John asked, as he walked into the kitchen.

"He's been in the bathroom most of the morning. His stomach is upset. . ."

"I'm right here," Samuel said, as he came into the room. "My stomach is fine."

"I thought you were gone," John said.

"And, just where do you think I'd go?"

"I don't know. Just some place, I guess," John answered. "

"My going someplace days are over," the old man replied. "Just let me get a cup of coffee and we'll get started."

"You go on, Grandpa. I'll bring you your coffee," Julia told him.

"Make sure it's good and hot, please."

The two boys settled in on the floor, waiting for Samuel to continue telling them his story. The old man looked at their young faces and sighed. What I wouldn't give to be that young again and have my whole life ahead of me, he thought.

"I stopped right after Mr. Jones reported his

daughter missing, didn't I?" he asked.

"Right," Whitey replied. "Then, what happened."

"Wait," John cried out. "We forgot to tell you something."

"What would that be?" Samuel asked.

"We went through the house. You know - the Pearys' house. Sarah Peary showed us around."

Samuel sat back in his chair and smiled. "How did you manage that?"

"We went right up to the door and rang the bell," Whitey responded.

"We didn't ring the bell," John corrected him. "We were going to, but Sarah was outside and we talked to her and she let us in."

"How does it look inside," Samuel asked.

"It's really a nice house. The woodwork is beautiful and there are some stained glass windows."

"You noticed all that, did you?" he asked John.

"We went up to the attic," Whitey said. "It was really hot up there. I can't believe that those kids had to sleep up there. Anyway, Sarah told us that her father didn't want anyone going up there, so we didn't spend a lot of time there. It's all open, anyway. There wasn't much to see. It's just one huge room with some boxes that are stored there. Sarah said that they were filled with Christmas stuff."

"Yeah. There really wasn't much to look at there," John chimed in.

"I asked her if she ever heard any strange noises coming from up there. You know, footsteps or moaning or anything. She said they didn't hear anything coming from the attic, but once in a while they heard noises coming from the basement."

"Really?" Samuel said.

"The basement gave me the creeps," John declared. "Sarah said she didn't like being down there. It's big. There are six rooms down there."

"I remember," Samuel commented.

"There's a trap door that goes outside. Sarah said her dad told her it was there so that the women could go right outside to hang up their wash."

"Did you see anyplace that could have been an opening to a tunnel that had been sealed off?" Samuel asked.

"No. But, Sarah said that there used to be a place in the back yard where there was another trap door. She showed us where it used to be, but it was all filled in and there was grass there. I guess that's the tunnel that you told us about, but you couldn't tell that it had ever been there."

"Well, it sounds like you boys had a good afternoon yesterday. I have to tell you, though. I don't think there was ever a tunnel there."

"What about that FBI guy that says he watched those crooks unload that truck? You said they. . ."

"I know what I said," Samuel said, interrupting John. "But, to be honest with you, it doesn't make a whole lot of sense. I think they unloaded the trucks over there, and then carried the booze through the back yard of the house next door, and down that trap door you saw. I can't prove it one way or the other, but that makes more sense to me."

Whitey looked over at John and shrugged. "It does make more sense, Poop."

"I guess," John agreed.

"Did you find anything unusual in that house while you were there?" Samuel asked.

"Nah. It's a nice house and all, but nothing that seemed strange.

"There was that one thing that Sarah showed us, though, that was different."

"What was that, John," Samuel asked.

"In that one room with the trap door, there was this big cement wall that didn't go all the way to the ceiling. Sarah said it was called a cistern and was used for holding rain water. But, it had been filled in with dirt or cement or something years ago. Anyway, she said that her dad was thinking of having it taken out."

"A lot of old houses have cisterns," Samuel told the boys. "And, she's right. They were used to catch rain water." He thought for a few moments. "You say it was filled in?"

"Yes, Sir," John replied.

"I wonder when that was done?" the old man said, quietly. He thought for a moment. "I wonder if that. . ." He hesitated. "Never mind. Okay, back to the story. Well, just like when poor Franny Franklin went missing, the town went wild. Every available man, including me, started searching for her. Every house, garage, and barn was searched from top to bottom."

"You searched, too?" John asked. "How old were you?"

Samuel smiled. "I guess I was around sixty or so. And, yes, I was part of the search party. That was thirty years ago, John. I was still able to get around just fine."

"I didn't mean anything," John said.

"I know, you didn't. We searched until it was too dark to see anything, and as soon as the sun was up the next morning, we were back at it. We finally gave up, when there was no place left to look. We didn't have much hope that Emily Jones would be found alive.

"About two weeks later, there was a party being held in the park pavilion. It might have been a wedding celebration, but I'm not sure about that. Well, it seems that a young man, who had a few too many drinks, wandered off to toss his cookies behind some bushes and stumbled onto Emily's body. Or, what was left of it, I should say. It was pretty obvious that she had only been there for a short time."

"Was she in a gunny sack, too?" Whitey asked.

"No, but it would have been better if she had been."

"Why's that?" John asked.

"Because, that young lady was buck naked and lying there for everyone to see. It was god awful. She had already started to rot, and there were maggots crawling out of her mouth and nose and most of her other holes. The young man who found her screamed for help and, suddenly, there were dozens of people looking at the poor dead girl. Some of the men were gagging, some were vomiting, and a number of the women, who saw the body, fainted. I'll tell you, boys, it was a real circus. Finally, the father of the bride. . ." Samuel paused. "That's right – it was a wedding party. Anyway, the father of the bride stepped up and took over and got everyone away from the body. He yelled

55

out, asking that someone call Police Chief Walker and report that they had found Emily's body and to get his ass out to the park as fast as possible."

"He's not in town," the young man, who found the body, told him.

"Where the hell is he?" the father of the bride asked. He looked at the young man and frowned. "You're Walker's son, aren't you? What's your name?"

"Yes, Sir, Chief Walker is my father. My name is Jacob. Jacob Walker. I suggest you call the police station. Someone should be there that can handle this situation."

"You call this a situation? We have a dead girl lying here and to you it's a situation?" The man stared at Jacob. "It was your brother, wasn't it? He did this, just like he killed Franny Franklin. Well, he's not going to get away with it this time. I'll see to it, even if I have to string him up myself."

"Sir, I can assure you that my brother had nothing to do with this."

"Says you." The man turned to the crowd that had gathered and yelled, "This is Jacob Walker. His brother killed Emily and we all know it. He killed her just like he killed Franny Franklin. Well, I, for one, am not letting that half-wit get away with it this time. Let's go find him and see that justice is done. Are you with me, men?"

"No!" Jacob yelled. "John Henry didn't do this. He's not even in. . ."

Suddenly, Jacob was pushed from behind and he fell to the ground. As he tried to get up, a man kicked him in the ribs. "You're making a mistake," Jacob cried out, as he was kicked again. "He's not in town. He's not here."

His words fell on deaf ears as the crowd, which had now turned into a lynch mob, ran out of the park, heading for the Walker house on North Ludington Street.

Jacob stood, trying to catch his breath, but the pain was too severe. He was sure that he had a least one broken rib. He managed to make it to a park bench and sat down, wondering what he should do. His grandmother was home alone and a mob was about to rain down on her. He needed to call her. He needed to call the police. He stood and painfully limped to the pavilion, hoping to reach the telephone before it was too late.

He made it to the phone and reached into his pocket. "No!" he cried out, as he realized he had no coins for the phone and he couldn't warn his grandmother in time.

An hour later, Jacob Walker stood on the porch of his home. Glass crunched under his feet as he walked through the open door into the house. The beautiful leaded glass window, that had adorned the door, had been shattered. "Grandmother?" he called out. "Grandmother? Where are you?"

He looked around the room. Some of the furniture had been overturned and table lamps were on the floor, broken. "Grandmother?" he cried out again.

Suddenly, he thought he heard a faint cry and he held his breath, hoping to determine where it came from. He heard the cry again and limped to the kitchen.

He opened the door that led to the cellar. "Grandmother?" he shouted. "Are you down there?"

"Jacob?" a voice called out.

He slowly made it down the stairs, afraid at what he might find. "No!" he yelled, as he turned the corner and entered the adjoining room. His grandmother was lying on her back on the cold cement floor. "What did they do to you?" he cried out.

"I didn't tell them," she said. "You would have been so proud of me, Jacob. No one will ever know."

Jacob dropped to his knees alongside of her and took her hand. "Which one hurt you?" he asked her.

The old woman slowly closed her eyes, expelled her last breath, and died.

Jacob took her in his arms, sobbing as he held her tight. "I promise they'll pay for this," he said, softly. "Every one of those bitches will be dead before I'm through."

You could have heard a pin drop, the room was so quiet,.

John, confused, looked at Samuel. "I don't get it," he finally said. "Do you get it, Whitey?"

Whitey shook his head up and down. "I think so. Jacob killed those two girls, not John Henry. Right, Mr. H?"

"That can't be right," John said. "Gramps?"

"Whitey's right. It was almost six months before the truth came out and Jacob was caught."

Samuel sat back in his chair, thinking. "I guess we could stop here for now," he finally said.

"No!" both boys shouted.

"Don't stop yet," John pleaded. "It's not even time for dinner yet."

Samuel smiled. "Well, I guess I can continue a little longer. But, first, I need a bathroom break."

Nine

"John Henry was an extremely good looking young man," Samuel said, after he had settled back down in his chair. "I guess you could say he was movie star good looking. Jacob, on the other hand, was ugly. His features just didn't go well together. Besides being short, he had small eyes that were set far back in the sockets and a nose that was way too small. His mouth slanted down a little, which made him look constantly angry. I think people might have overlooked all of this, but it was his personality that was extremely off putting. He was a nasty bastard. As far as I know, he didn't have any friends. The girls, that had gone to school with him, hated him and did their best to stay clear of him. "

"Unfortunately, he murdered two more of these girls before he was caught. Mary Lou Helwig and Monica Roche were their names. It eventually came out that these murdered girls had turned him down when he had asked them for dates. They didn't just tell him 'no thank you' when they refused his invitation. No, they were nasty little teenage girls who told basically him they would rather be dead than go out with him. I recall being told that he laughed and said, 'well, they got their wish, didn't they?' while he was confessing to the police."

"How'd they catch him?" Whitey inquired.

"He got sloppy. Remember, he was still only working part time for the town and had a lot of time on his hands. It came out, after the fact, of course, that he used to stand on the corner across from the school and watch the girls. He'd follow them after school let out and wait for an opportunity to grab them. He'd stick a knife in their backs and threaten to kill them if they screamed. I still can't believe no one saw him walking with any of them. Anyway, he would take them to his house and hide them in the basement."

"His dad was a cop," John exclaimed. "How did he get away with that?"

"You were in that basement. Did you see any places where you could keep a body?" Samuel asked.

Whitey looked at John and shrugged. "I don't know. I guess. There is that room with the cistern and the door that goes outside, and the room where you come down the stairs. I don't think those would be a good place to hide anyone."

"The two middles rooms probably wouldn't work either," John said, chiming in.

"But, the two back rooms would," Whitey declared.

"Yeah," John agreed. "That one room was really a lot colder than the others. There were a lot of shelves with canned goods on them. Sarah said that before her mother left the shelves would always be full of canned stuff. Now, there are only a few dusty jars of pickles that have been there for a long time."

"That room is called a cold cellar," Samuel told him. "And, because it is colder than the other rooms, it would be a perfect place to store a body. Plus, it seems that Jacob killed the girls almost immediately after he took them. He'd cover their bodies with a tarp of some kind and wait until the odor got so bad he was afraid his father would smell it upstairs. Then, he'd sneak

61

them out in the middle of the night and put them where they would be found."

"His grandmother knew, didn't she?" John asked the old man.

"She did. The old lady must have been a little off her rocker to go along with it. She knew what her grandson was doing, but she never said anything. I guess she figured she had one grandson who was slow and she didn't need to let the world know that she had another one who was nuts. Anyway, like I said, Jacob got sloppy. He waited at school like usual. However, this time, when he came up behind his next intended victim and threatened her with a knife, the girl turned and kicked him right in his nuts."

"What?" Whitey cried out, laughing. "You're kidding?"

"Nope. That's what happened. She screamed as loud as she could as she kicked him, and a couple of high school boys came running to help her. Jacob was rolling on the ground in pain and one of the boys sat on him while the other got the knife out of his hand."

"Later, when the girl told the cops what he had said to her, they knew they had their killer. Police Chief Walker excused himself from the case and quit his job. Within a month he had left town. Jacob was tried for murder and was sentenced to hang, but he killed himself in prison before the sentence was carried out."

"What happened to John Henry?" Whitey asked.

"No idea," Samuel replied. "Okay, boys. That's it for today."

"What about this afternoon?" John asked him.

62

He hesitated. "Sorry. No, that's it for today."

"Who lived there next?" John inquired.

"Let's save that for tomorrow," Samuel told him.

The boys stood and stretched. "This is really interesting," John told Samuel.

"I'm glad you're enjoying it," the old man said.

As Whitey and John started to leave the room, Whitey turned to John and whispered, "Yeah, but are we ever going to find out if there's a tunnel under City Hall?"

"I can hear you," Samuel called out.

"Where are you going?" John asked Whitey.

"Home. My mom has things for me to do."

"Are you coming over later?" John inquired.

"I don't think so." Whitey looked over at John's mom and waved. "Bye, Mrs. H. Thanks for dinner."

"You're welcome, Whitey," she replied.

John watched his leave and turned to his mom. "I think I'll take a nap."

Mrs. Hassel stared at him. "Are you feeling okay?"

"I guess. I just feel like taking a nap. You know. Like Gramps does after he has dinner."

Mrs. Hassel shook her head. "I think you might be spending altogether too much time with him, John."

"John! John, wake up," Julia Hassel shouted. She gently shook his shoulder. "John," she said again, softer this time.

John rolled over and opened his eyes. "Wha? Whatsa' matter?"

"Are you okay?" his mother asked. "You were yelling."

John rubbed his eyes and sat up. He gave his mother a confused look and shook his head. "I'm fine. It was just a bad dream."

"It must have been a really bad one," Julia commented. "I've never heard you yell like that."

"Sorry."

"Do you want to talk about it?"

"Nah. It was just a dream," John said.

"I think those stories about those murders are freaking you out."

John laughed. "What makes you think I was dreaming about that stuff?"

"Well, do you know anyone else named Jacob except the one that used to live in that damn house?"

John threw the ball and turned to face Whitey, a big grin on his face. "A strike, isn't it?"

Whitey watch the ball hit the pins and made a disgusted face. "You got lucky."

"Luck, hell. I'm just good and you know it." He reached down and started to untie his bowling shoes. "You want to get a hamburger or something at Earl's?"

"I guess," Whitey replied. "I'm short on change, though."

"My treat," John said. "Remind me to tell you about a nightmare I had this afternoon."

"Why would you have a nightmare in the middle of the day?" Whitey asked him.

"I was tired, so I took a nap."

Whitey laughed. "Who are you? Your Grampa?"

64

The two boys handed in their bowling shoes, left the bowling alley, and started walking the few blocks to the café. Whitey picked up a penny that was lying on the sidewalk. "Good luck," he commented, as he put it in his pocket.

"You got any of those cigs left?"

"I thought you were trying to quit," Whitey said.

"I am. I just feel like having one right now."

"Sorry, I'm all out, Whitey told him.

"You smoke too much."

Whitey shrugged. "No more than most people. So, Poop, what was that nightmare all about?"

"I don't remember all of it" John said. "For some reason, I was in the basement and I was. . ."

"What basement?" Whitey interrupted.

"You know, Sarah's basement. I was really cold and I couldn't see anything. I realized that my whole body was covered with something. At first, I thought I was in a sleeping bag, because my movements were restricted, but it wasn't soft enough. I started to yell, but I stopped when I heard footsteps coming towards me. I heard a voice say, 'So, you're finally awake, are you?' Then, I felt someone touch me and I heard a zipper noise and felt the cold air on my face. I realized I was in a body bag like they use for dead people. 'Who are you?' I cried out. 'What's happening?' There was hardly any light in the room, but I could make out a figure standing over me."

"How'd you get in the basement?" Whitey asked, interrupting John.

John gave Whitey an exasperated look. "How

should I know?"

"What? You're in a basement and you don't know how you got there?"

John, looking annoyed, stopped walking. "It was a dream. Do you want to hear this or not?"

Whitey grinned. "Just pulling your leg, Poop. Please, continue."

"No more interruptions. Got it?"

"Go," Whitey said.

"The figure was holding something and when the light shined on it, I realized it was a knife. As I tried to get up, the figure put its foot on my chest and pushed me back down. 'Not today. Not any day,' it whispered. Then, it laughed this horrible laugh. It wasn't really so much as a laugh as it was a cackle Like a witch's laugh, I guess."

"Wow!" Whitey stated. "That's really scary. Not!"

John ignored him and said. "The figure bent down, raised the knife, and plunged it into my chest. It was then that I saw its face. It was Jacob Walker's grandmother. As she raised the knife and stabbed me again, I cried out, pleading with her to stop. She looked me straight in the eyes and I watched as one of her tears fell onto my cheek. 'I can't' she said, softly. As I lay on the cold, damp floor in that cold cellar, dying, I watched her face metamorphose and she became Sarah. I started to scream. . ."

Whitey stopped walking and looked at John.

"What?" John asked.

"Metamo what?" he said, loudly. "What the hell is that?"

"I'm sorry," John said. "I forgot who I was talking

66

to. Change, Whitey. It means change."

"Just keep it real, will you?"

"Right."

Whitey grinned, as he asked, "How do you know what that old grandmother looked like, anyway?"

John shook his head and sighed. "So, I've decided that I'm going to ask Sarah out on a date."

Grabbing his chest and moaning, Whitey did an exaggerated fall to the sidewalk. "Oh, no," he cried out. "Not a date. Now, that's what I call a real nightmare."

Ten

"The house stayed empty for years. It was finally put up for sale in the spring of 1930. Painters were hired to give it a new coat of paint on the outside and decorators wallpapered the rooms inside. The bank, who once again owned it, had cleaning women scrubbing it from top to bottom. All the old furniture, which had been collecting dust for years, was loaded onto the large porch and given away to people for free."

Samuel pointed at a beautiful old cherry wood dresser that was in his bedroom. "You see that?" he asked the two boys. "I got that dresser from that porch. It used to be in Henry Walker's bedroom." He gazed at it for a moment. "Beautiful, isn't it?"

Whitey shrugged. "I guess so. It looks like any other old dresser to me."

"Maybe someday, when you're older, you'll appreciate a piece of work like that. What about you, John?"

John looked over at Samuel and smiled. "It's nice enough, but I'm not really into furniture."

"Nooo. He's not." Whitey said, laughing. "He's into Sarah Peary."

"What's that?" Samuel asked. "You have a girlfriend, John?"

"Shut up, Whitey," John said, turning red. "Don't pay him any attention, Gramps. Go on."

Samuel chuckled and dropped the subject of Sarah Peary. "Anyway, the lawn was mowed and the bushes and flowers were tended to, and, once again, that house looked beautiful. The bank put a For Sale sign in the window and everyone waited to see who would be living there next."

"Now, remember, that house had a horrible history. From the time it was built until 1930, there had been. . ." Samuel held up his left hand and started counting on his fingers. "I forgot there were so many," he said, quietly. He looked down at the boys, who were sitting on the floor. "Seven killed in that house." He shook his head. "No, eight. I almost forgot Jacob Walker's grandmother. And, three people who lived there committed suicide."

"Don't forget Von Schmidt's wife," John said. "She went missing, didn't she? She could have died there, too."

"And, Sarah's mother," Whitey chimed in. "Does anyone know where she is?"

Samuel and John both stared at him.

"She's not missing," Samuel finally stated. "I don't think we can add her to this equation."

"Well, it's been years since anyone has seen her, hasn't it?" Whitey asked.

"We're getting off topic, Whitey," Samuel said. He let out a sigh and sat back. "All right. Back to 1930. The house had plenty of lookers for the first couple of months. But, with its history and all, no one put an offer on it. Then, towards the end of September, the town was buzzing with the news that the house had been sold to a family from down south. And, when I say down south, I mean way down south. Like, Louisiana south. You can get much further south than that."

"I'll never forget that day," Samuel said, smiling.

"When I saw that woman for the first time, my heart skipped a beat. I was between wives at that time, and I remember thinking how she might be my number three. God, she was beautiful." The old man looked over at the window and grinned.

"Why are you smiling?" Whitey asked.

Samuel looked down at him. "I guess thinking about her makes me happy. Sometimes, I wonder if I had. . ." His voice trailed off.

"Anyway," he continued, "I just happened to be at the depot when the train pulled in. I don't remember why I was there." He thought for a moment. "Hell, it's not important. Anyway, the train door opened and this beautiful woman held out her hand to the conductor. I watched as he helped her step off the train. She was so graceful; almost swan like. And, following her, just like a mother swan with her cygnets, were four gorgeous young ladies. Columbus suddenly seemed a lot brighter that day."

"You looved her," John said, and started making kissing sounds. "You wanted to marry her."

Whitey laughed. "You wanted her to have your babies," he added.

Samuel smiled. "Yes, I did. For about five minutes."

"Why only five minutes?" John inquired.

"Because, right after the last young lady exited the train, a huge man stepped off right behind her, who I assumed was her husband. I watched him say something to the mother swan, who shook her head and started walking the short block to her new house. The girls followed her, each carrying a small bag, while the man stayed behind to gather up the rest of the luggage. I don't know how the word spread so fast, but within minutes, there were all these people walking towards the depot." Samuel smiled. "It was really quite a sight to see. All those people, acting like they were out for a stroll, while it was obvious that they were there to check her out."

"And, then, she did something that I will never forget. Rose Scarborough - that was her name. Rose walked up the steps onto the porch, turned, and looked out at the crowd. By now, it actually was a crowd. She turned and said, 'How do you do. I'm Rose Scarborough and I'm so glad to meet y'all. I'd like you to meet my daughters'. . .'" Samuel glanced down at a piece of paper he was holding. "Sorry, I had to write their names down," he told the boys. "She said, 'these are my daughters, Ada Mae, Azelea, Charlotte, and Pearl. We hope y'all be visiting us as soon as we get settled in and enjoy a nice cup of tea with us.' By now, everyone had quit pretending they were out for a leisurely stroll and were standing in front of the house, staring at her and her daughters."

"Are all those ladies your daughters?" a man called out.

Rose smiled at the man. "They sure are, sweetie.
"Even the black one?" another voice yelled.

"What?" John cried out. "No way!"

"Yessiree Bob," Samuel said. "It looked like the first black person had moved to Columbus, with her white mother and sisters. That caused a little bit of a

71

stir, I can tell you. Well, that big fellow, who had been collecting the luggage at the depot, showed up just then. He walked up onto the porch and over to where Rose and her girls were and stared out at the crowd. 'The show is over, folks,' he yelled, as he took Rose's arm, and escorted her into her new home."

Samuel yawned. "And, this show is over for now. It's break time," Samuel said, as he stood up and stretched.

"About a week or so later, a small advertisement appeared in the Republican Journal promoting the Scarborough Tea House, open Monday through Friday from ten to two. The ad indicated that there would be many different flavors of tea to choose from, traditional sandwiches, and a variety of cakes."

"When I read that ad, I remember thinking that the Scarborough Tea House would be out of business within the month. Man, was I wrong. The women, who could afford it, frequented the tea house, often staying two or three hours. Rose set up one room where little children were watched by one of her daughters – for a fee of course - while the mothers enjoyed their tea time without being disturbed."

Samuel chuckled, as he thought about what he was going to say next. "Rose did real well with her afternoon teas. She did even better, though, with those private events she held a few times a month."

"I'd like to see Mayor Dering, please," Rose said, in a quiet voice. She looked at the name plate on the woman's desk. "Are you Mabel?"

72

The mayor's receptionist looked up from her desk and frowned. "Of course, I am. Why else would I be sitting here? Do you have an appointment?"

Rose, looking slightly confused, shook her head. "I don't. I wasn't aware that I would need one to see him."

"Well, Mrs. . . I'm sorry. I didn't get your name."

Rose smiled at her. "Of course, you didn't. I'm the one that should be sorry. I'm Rose Scarborough. We just moved into that big house on Ludington Street."

"Oh, yes. You're the one with all those daughters."

Rose looked the woman up and down. "I must say, Mabel, that is a beautiful brooch. It so does compliment the green of your eyes."

Mabel's face lit up. "Why thank you. It was my mother's."

"Has she passed?"

"A year ago, already," Mabel told her.

"I am so sorry for your loss."

"Thank you. And, welcome to our little town, Mrs. Scarborough. I hope you'll be happy here."

"Why, thank you, dear. I do believe I will be." Rose brushed back a lock of hair that had fallen over her forehead. *"So, is the mayor here?"*

"He is, but he's busy. Besides, you do need an appointment to see him. I'd be glad to make one for you." The receptionist looked down at an appointment book and started flipping some of the pages. *"I have something next week, if that is convenient for you."*

Rose, looking very unhappy, glanced over the receptionists shoulder and suddenly smiled. "Why, I do

*believe that's the mayor sitting right there in that office."
She walked by the startled woman and pushed the
door the rest of the way open. "Good morning, Mayor
Dering. My name is Rose Scarborough, and I'd be so
grateful if you could give me a few moments of your
time."*

*The receptionist, running through the door behind
her, yelled, "Mrs. Scarborough, you can't go in there!"*

*Mayor Dering looked up at Rose and, then, over
at his receptionist. "It's fine, Mabel."*

*"But, she doesn't have an appointment," Mabel
exclaimed.*

*"Rose, I said that it's fine. Please make sure we
aren't interrupted and I'd appreciate it if you would
close the door on your way out," Mayor Dering said,
never taking his eyes off of Rose's face.*

"But..."

"Out!" he said, practically yelling. "Now!"

*As soon as Mabel closed the office door, Mayor
Dering stood and walked over to where Rose was
standing and took her hand. "Please excuse my
receptionist. She was just trying to do her job."*

*"Well, of course, she was. And, it's I that should
be asking to be excused. It's just that when I saw you
through that half open door, I just knew I couldn't wait
another minute to meet you."*

*"I'm flattered," he said, letting go of her hand. "I
must say that it is a pleasure to meet you. Please, have
a seat," he said, gesturing towards a chair in front of
his desk.*

*"Why, thank you, Sir," Rose practically purred, as
she sat down.*

74

The mayor sat on the edge of his desk, facing her. "What can I do for you, Mrs. Scarborough?" he asked.

"No, no. Please, call me Rose," she said.

Dering smiled. "Of course. And, I'd appreciate it if you called me Russell."

"Why, Mr. Mayor Russell Dering, I'd be honored to."

Dering laughed. "That was quite a mouthful, but Russell will do."

Rose crossed her legs, managing to hike her skirt up just enough to show some leg. "I have a proposition for you," she declared, smiling.

"They made their deal. Rose turned one of the upstairs bedrooms into a poker room. Cards and booze. Men do love their cards and liquor. She did everything just right and the money poured in. She was selling her poker playing clients some of the finest whiskey money could buy and she was charging an arm and a leg for it. Remember, prohibition was still going on, and what she was doing was as illegal as all get out. The Mayor handpicked a select group of men, who met a few times a month to play poker. They were sworn to secrecy and it was months – maybe a year - before the town found out what was going on. The Mayor, on the other hand, got a sizable cut of everything. Well, not from the income from Rose's tea room, of course. That all went to Rose and her girls. With his cut, Mayor Dering paid off the police to look the other way. Everyone was happy; at least for a while."

"Did you ever go there, Gramps?" John asked

Samuel.

Samuel looked at him, a big smile on his face. "I was tempted. But, I heard that the stakes were pretty high and I knew I couldn't afford playing in those games. You couldn't go there just to drink. That privilege was reserved for the poker players. However, I did go there one time to fix something for Rose."

"What was that?" Whitey asked.

"A rod in her closet needed to be fixed. It didn't take long and, after I finished, she offered me a cup of tea and we talked in the kitchen for a while. She was real nice to me and she paid me right away."

"You looved her," Whitey sang out, and started making kissing sounds.

Samuel grinned. "Enough. You did that already. It was a little funny the first time. Now, it's just stupid."

Eleven

"Now, selling booze during the prohibition was a serious offense. Quite a few people made what they called bathtub gin, which was mostly just for themselves to drink. The feds pretty much looked the other way in those situations. They concentrated more on the big shots, like Capone and Bugsy Siegel."

"Wait." John said. "What's bathtub gin?"

"It's a mixture of cheap grain alcohol and some fruit, such as juniper berries. Mostly, it was mixed in large cans, but some people actually made it in their bathtubs, hence, the name. It was horrible stuff. A lot of people died from drinking it."

"Did you ever drink it?" Whitey asked.

Samuel faked a shocked look. "Of course not," he said, holding back a smile. "It was illegal. I would never break the law."

John laughed. "Yeah, right. You were always a perfect angel."

"I was," Samuel agreed. "Anyway, Mayor Dering got greedy. He liked the extra money that Rose's business was bringing his way, but he didn't like having to split his share with the cops in town. He decided it was time to have a chat with Rose and discuss their business arrangement. It was a beautiful day outside, so he walked the few blocks from City Hall to Rose's house. Just as he was about to ring the bell, Buck threw open the front door, surprising him."

"Who is Buck?" Whitey interrupted.

Samuel looked at him, confused. "You know. Buck. I told you about him."

"I don't remember that," John said, looking at Whitey. "Do you remember?"

"I'm not sure," Whitey replied. "Refresh my memory."

"Buck was Rose's brother."

"Ah, that's right," John said, pretending to remember. "The big guy from the train. You remember, don't you, Whitey?"

Whitey slapped his forehead. "Of course. Sorry, Mr. H. It slipped my mind."

Samuel grinned. "And, I thought I was the one who had CRS."

"Mayor Dering," Buck acknowledged, as he opened the door. "I didn't know you had an appointment to see Miss Rose this morning."

"Morning, Buck," Dering said, smiling. "Why, you know right well that Rose and I don't need appointments to see each other. Is she in?"

"She's busy in her tea room, seeing to her guests' needs. This really isn't a good time," Buck informed him.

Mayor Dering pulled out his pocket watch and checked the time. "When is a good time, then? I do need to talk to her as soon as possible."

"Is it something that I can help you with?" Buck asked him.

Mayor Dering shook his head no. "I doubt it, Buck, but thanks for asking. Tell Rose I'll be back around two to talk to her."

"I think three-thirty would be better. Some of the ladies have a tendency to stay a little longer after

closing time."

"Fine. I'll be back at three-thirty, then," Mayor Dering said, as he turned and started down the porch steps.

"Mayor?" Buck called to him.

Dering turned and looked at him. "What now?" he asked, irritated that he had made a wasted trip.

"You might want to walk the other way, unless you don't care if Mrs. Dering sees you leaving here."

"What difference would that make?" John asked Samuel. "If she saw him, I mean."

"Well, it's one thing for Mrs. Dering to be there for a cup of tea or some type of refreshment. But, if she saw her husband leaving the house, she might wonder what he was doing there. Certainly, not getting a cup of tea. Remember, she didn't know about the agreement between him and Rose. He'd have some explaining to do that might not go so well. So, it was best that she didn't see him."

"Right," John agreed. "That makes sense."

"I'm so glad you agree," Samuel said, holding back a smile.

At three o'clock, Mayor Dering rang the doorbell. Buck answered the door and frowned. "I thought we agreed on three-thirty," he said, obviously irritated at Dering's early arrival.

"I thought you said three," Dering replied. "Can I see her now?"

"Come in and have a seat," Buck said. He motioned to the living room. "I'll let her know you're

here."

Rose kept the mayor waiting for twenty minutes. Getting angrier by the minute, he was about to walk out the door when she hurried into the living room. "I am so, so sorry," she said in her soft voice. "It gets pretty busy here sometimes, and I can't just kick my clients out at the stroke of two." She smiled sweetly at him. "Am I forgiven?" she asked.

"My dear, I could never be angry with you," he said, taking her hand and kissing it.

"That's good to know," she commented, as she pulled her hand back. "Now, just what is so important that it couldn't wait until tomorrow?"

"How many of those daughters of yours are actually your daughters?" Mayor Dering blurted out.

Rose's head jerked up and she stared at him. "Exactly what are you getting at? They all are my daughters."

"Even Pearl?" Dering inquired with a smirk on his face. "And, Rose darling, before you answer me, I think you should know that I talked to the Chief of Police in Baton Rouge."

Rose turned and looked out the front window. "It certainly is a beautiful day. And, now here you are, trying to ruin it for me."

"No, no," Dering told her. "I'm not doing anything of the sort. I'm here to make it better for you."

"For me or for you?" Rose asked, angrily.

"Well, I guess you could say for both of us. You've got those girls waiting on tables and serving tea while they could be making us a fortune doing what they do so well. I guarantee you won't be run out of town here

like you were down in Baton Rouge."

"I'm out of that business. And, so are the girls. We agreed, when we moved up north, that we were going to put that life behind us," Rose told him.

"You've got four beautiful women here who could be making us a fortune. I think you better think about it, Rose, if you want to stay in business."

Rose stared at him. "That sounds like a threat, Russell."

"Well, I didn't mean it that way, but I guess it just might be. What do you say?"

"If I did consider it, what do you want out of it?"

"Half. That seems fair to me, seeing as how I have to pay off the Police Chief."

"You're kidding? We are supposed to do all the work and you want fifty percent? That's crazy. No way. I'll leave town first," she yelled.

"No, you won't. I'll have you arrested for selling alcohol before I'll let you leave this town. You'll wind up in jail along with your brother and all your so called daughters."

"And, I'll tell everyone in town that it was your idea and you supplied all that liquor," Rose shouted back at him. "And, that your wife is a drunk," she added.

The door to the room suddenly opened, surprising them.

"Are you okay?" Buck asked his sister.

Mayor Dering glanced over at Buck and laughed. "Of course, she's okay. It's just a heated discussion between friends."

"Rose, do you need any help?" Buck asked.

"I'm fine. The Mayor is being a little unreasonable, that's all. I'll call you if I need you," she told Buck.

She waited until Buck left the room, then, turned and faced Dering.

"Twenty-five percent. Not a penny more," she stated emphatically.

"Forty," Dering said.

"Thirty. And, that's it."

"Done," Dering said, smiling. "When do you think you'll get started?"

Rose looked at him and shook her head in disgust. "Aren't you the greedy one."

"The sooner the better," Dering told her.

"I suppose I could be ready in a few weeks. I've got some decorating to do first. And, I guess I'll have to close down the tea room. I can't expect the girls to work both jobs."

"No. You need to keep the tea room open," Dering told her, emphatically. "Hire a few women to work it."

"Absolutely not," Rose said. "I don't want any outsiders working here. I'll try to work something out."

"We're set then," Dering remarked. He hesitated a moment, then asked, "What did you mean when you called my wife a drunk?"

"Nothing," Rose said. "I was just being nasty, that's all."

"Are you serving more than tea here in your tea room, Rose? Because, if you are, it looks like we might need to discuss that, too."

"I'm not selling it, so put your greedy hand back in your pocket. A couple of the ladies like a drink now *and then, so I provide it for them. It just seems that I'm providing more for Mrs. Dering than any of the others."*

Mayor Dering smiled. "I thought she seemed a lot more mellow since you came to town. Just make sure she doesn't overdo it, okay? I'd hate to think she'd be known as our town drunk."

"I'm not happy about this new deal, you know?" Rose said.

"You'll sing a different tune when the money starts rolling in," Dering said.

"Buck!" Rose yelled. "Come and see Mayor Dering out, please."

"Would you call Grandpa and the boys to dinner?" Julia Hassel asked her husband.

"Doesn't it seem strange to you?" Isaac asked Julia.

"What's that?"

"Summer is almost over and school is going to begin in a few weeks and those two boys are spending all their time with Grandpa. It just doesn't seem right somehow."

"He is passing history on to those boys. I've listened in a few times and it's really interesting. I never knew some of the stuff he's telling them. And, I'd much rather they be here where I know what they're doing than running around getting into trouble," Julia said.

"I guess," Isaac said. He chuckled.

"What?" Julia asked him.

"I can remember when I was little and Grandpa told me stories. He certainly had a way with words."

"I'm just surprised he can remember all that stuff. He can't remember what he had for breakfast, but he remembers what happened all those years ago," Julia said.

"That sounds about right. Isn't that that usually happens when people grow old?" Isaac inquired.

"Sadly, it does," Julia replied. "Will you tell them dinner is ready?"

"John! Whitey! Grandpa! Dinner!" Isaac shouted.

Julia looked at him and shook her head. "I could have done that," she muttered.

"Is it your nap time?" John asked Samuel.

Samuel laid his fork on his plate and wiped his mouth with his napkin. "You know it is," Samuel replied.

"So, what do you plan on doing this afternoon?" Julia asked her son.

John shrugged. "Nothing special. Might go to the park and hang around for a while."

Whitey pushed his chair back from the table. "Thanks for dinner, Mrs. H."

"You're welcome, Whitey."

Whitey looked over at Samuel.

"What? You want something?" Samuel asked him.

"When you were telling us about Rose and Mayor Dering, what did you. . ." He looked confused. "I'm not sure what you meant. . ."

"You're not sure what I meant about what, Whitey?" Samuel asked.

"What did Mayor Dering mean when he said

84

Rose's girls could do what they do so well? I think I know, but I'm not sure. He meant they were whores. Right?"

"No." John said, laughing. "He meant they were Sunday school teachers."

Samuel grinned. "You hit the nail right on the head, Whitey."

Julia looked at Samuel and frowned. "I don't know if I like you talking to the boys about that kind of stuff," she declared.

"Ah, Mom. We know all about that stuff. Right, Whitey?"

"We sure do," Whitey said. "My dad had 'the talk' with me a long time ago."

Julia glanced over at Isaac. "Have you had 'the talk' with John?" she asked, grinning.

"Well, I don't - I mean, I plan to - I'm not exactly sure. . ." he mumbled.

John laughed. "That's okay, Dad. I'm good. Whitey told me all about it."

"Isaac?"

"Yes, dear."

"I think it might be a good idea if you took some time and reviewed this subject with John."

"Ah, Mom," John said. "He doesn't have to do that."

Whitey looked at Isaac and raised his hand. "Mr. H?"

Isaac laughed. "Why are you raising your hand?"

"I have a question," Whitey told him.

"You don't have to raise your hand. You aren't in school, for goodness sake," Julia told him. "Just ask your question."

"Well," Whitey said, hesitating. "Well, I wonder if I could sit in on that talk. There are a few things I'm not sure about."

Isaac sat back and thought for a moment. "I think it would be better if you talked to your father about this subject, Whitey."

"I guess. But, it's some of the things he told me that I'm confused about."

Twelve

"*What kind of a cut is the mayor giving you?*" Rose asked, as she handed Police Chief Worthers a drink.

As he took the glass from her, Worthers grinned. "*Why, Mrs. Scarborough, shame on you. You know I don't discuss the going-ons between me and the mayor.*"

"*Wallace, I've asked you a hundred times to call me Rose. Mrs. Scarborough sounds so formal. Please?*"

Worthers chuckled. "*You sure know how to pour it on, don't you? Tell me, Rose, why are you so curious?*" he asked, emphasizing her name.

"*I'm just wondering if you're getting your fair share, is all. Especially now, with the Mayor wanting me to start this new business and all.*"

Worthers, totally serious now, stared at her. "*Just what business are you talking about?*" he asked.

"*Before we discuss that, let's review what's going on now. I'm paying Mayor Dering forty percent of my income from the poker games and the drink sales. He told me that he has to pay out twenty percent to you. I'm going to show you the figures, Wallace, and you tell me if you're getting your fair share.*"

"*I trust that Russell wouldn't cheat me, Rose. I don't need to look at your figures.*"

Rose opened an accounting ledger and pushed it across the table to Worthers. "*Are you sure?*"

The police chief started to push the ledger back towards her and stopped. He looked at an open page and, then, looked up at Rose.

"Take your time, Wallace," she told him. "I think you'll find it more than interesting."

He pulled the ledger closer, examining the entries.

Rose walked over to the stove, picked up the coffee pot and poured herself another cup of coffee. "Would you like another drink?" she asked, softly.

"I'm good," the police chief muttered, and kept studying the pages of the ledger. "Son of a bitch!" he finally exclaimed. "That son of a bitch!" He looked up at Rose. "How did you know?"

"I figured you were getting cheated," Rose stated. "Did you know he came to me a few weeks ago and asked me – no, he pretty much demanded – that I set up a house of ill repute? He wants my girls to become prostitutes."

Worthers looked shocked. "He didn't say anything to me about it."

"He wanted fifty percent of the take, but I talked him down and he agreed on thirty. I went along with it, Wallace, because if I didn't agree to his terms, he said he'd see us all in jail. He's blackmailing me and I don't know what to do," Rose said, tears filling her eyes. "I don't want to put my girls to work whoring themselves. Can you. . ." She put her face in her hands and started sobbing. "I'm so. . . I'm sorry. . ."

Police Chief Worthers reached over and took her hand and patted it. "Now, now," he said. "Don't you worry your pretty little head about this. I'll take care of everything for you."

Rose looked at him, trying to smile. "But, how? I've already done everything I can to stall him."

Police Chief Wallace Worthers sat back in his chair and smiled. "You know, Rose, If he was out of the picture I could. . ."

"You could what?" Rose asked, knowing what was coming next.

"Well, instead of you paying him, how would you feel about paying me instead?

"How would that work? I mean, surely Russell wouldn't go along with that," she said, looking confused.

"Maybe, Russell doesn't have a say in the matter," Worthers said, smirking. "Maybe, our mayor is due for some time off. A long time off."

"And, the forty percent is still a good figure for you?" Rose asked.

"I like it," Worthers said, grinning. "In fact, I like it a lot."

"And, I can forget about the whoring?"

Worthers sat back in his chair, thinking. "You can, if you agree to one thing," he said, after a few moments.

"Which is?" Rose slowly asked.

"I'd like one night a month with Pearl," he said, blushing slightly.

"Why Chief Worthers. I'm surprised at you. Aren't you a married man?"

"No, Rose, I'm not. And, before you answer, I should tell you that I know about Baton Rouge."

"I'm surprised he told you about that."

"Yes, but that's all he told me. He didn't tell me about his latest arrangement with you, which was a big mistake."

"What if Pearl doesn't agree to this?" Rose asked.

"Oh, I don't think that's gonna be a problem," Worthers declared. *"I'm pretty sure you can convince her. In fact, I think you can probably convince anyone to do anything you want."*

"The plan went like clockwork," Samuel told the boys. "A few days after Chief Worthers and Rose made their agreement, the Mayor received a letter informing him that he and his wife had won a six day trip to New York. The only catch was that the prize had to be used by the end of the month. The Mayor, who didn't want to pass up a free trip, immediately made arrangements to leave the following week. He had Mabel reschedule all his appointments, and a few days later the mayor and his wife were on their way."

Samuel turned his head away and cleared his throat. "Sorry. Guess I have a frog in my throat," he said, and started to cough.

"I'll get you a glass of water," John told him, as he jumped up and ran into the kitchen.

"Are you okay?" Whitey asked, after a few moments.

Samuel shook his head up and down and reached for the glass of water that John handed him. He took a long swallow and set the glass down. "I'm fine," he told Whitey. "Too much talking, I guess."

John, looking concerned, asked, "Do you want to stop for today?"

Samuel smiled. "I'm fine, John." He took another drink and sat back in his chair. "Anyway, to continue. The mayor and his wife were dropped off at the train depot to catch a train to Chicago. From there, they were to transfer to a train that would take them to New York. Everything was paid for. The train fares which included a private stateroom, their meals, the hotel in New York, plus tickets to a Broadway show. Everything. Now, I ask you, who could have turned that down?"

"I guess. . ." Whitey started to say.

"Never mind, Whitey. That was a rhetorical question," the old man said, interrupting before Whitey could finish his sentence."

"Oh," Whitey said. He glanced over at John and mouthed the words, "What's rhetorical mean?"

Samuel, who had seen Whitey, smiled. "John, see that dictionary on that shelf over there? Give it to Whitey, will you? He can look up the meaning when we're through here."

John laughed. "Sure thing, Gramps."

"Yes, Whitey, the answer is no one. This was a trip of a life time and even though Dering was Mayor of Columbus, he wasn't rich. Oh, he was well off, but only because of what he was pulling in from Rose's establishment. No, he had to be careful about spending money. If he took a trip like this using his own money, the town would be talking. But, to win a trip like this was. . . Well, the town couldn't have been more excited for him and his wife. So, their friends saw them off at the train station, wished them a good trip, and waved good bye. Six days later, when the train pulled into the station, they weren't on it. Then, seven days went by. Then, eight days. Elroy Jetson, the mayor's neighbor, finally made a trip to the police station and reported that he was pretty sure the mayor and his wife were missing."

Samuel laughed. "That damn Worthers waited a couple more days before he went through the pretense of trying to find out what had happened to the Derings. His first call was to the hotel in New York where the Derings had reservations. The manager there informed him that they had never arrived at the hotel, and suggested that he call the police. Worthers did just that. He gave the New York cops a description of the couple, and sat back and waited."

"Waited for what?" John asked.

"I figure he waited for their bodies to be found," Samuel said. "It took a while but eventually the news arrived that a couple of bodies, which had been found in a burned out car in Illinois, had been identified as Mayor Dering and his wife."

"Wow!" Whitey exclaimed. "Did they ever find out who killed them?"

"It's obvious, don't you think?" John said. "That cop, Worthers, had them killed so he could get all the money and not have to split it with the mayor. Isn't that right, Gramps?"

"Well, down the road, that's what everyone figured had happened. But, right there and then, no one had a clue."

"So, what happened to Rose? Did she ever open up that house of ill repute?" John asked, grinning.

"No, she didn't," Samuel told him. "She continued to run her tea house for the ladies in town and her poker games for the gentlemen. Her business flourished, especially the tea house and she eventually rented a store downtown and moved the tea house there.

"And, Pearl? Did she mess around with that cop like he wanted?" Whitey asked.

"You're getting ahead of the story," Samuel told them. "You're going to have to wait until tomorrow to hear any more." He started coughing again, and took a sip of water. "I'm tired, boys. I need to stop now."

"All right, Gramps," John said, as he stood up.

"Yeah, I'll see you tomorrow. Just one thing," Whitey said, hesitating.

"What's that, Whitey?" Samuel asked him.

"How do you spell rhetorical?"

Thirteen

"I'm afraid you and Whitey are going to have to find something else to do today," Julia told her son. "Grandpa isn't feeling well. I'm taking him to the doctor this morning."

"He sounded really bad yesterday, with that coughing and all. I hope we didn't wear him out," John commented.

"I don't think that's it," Julia told him. "He gets plenty of sleep. It's just that he's getting old, John. Telling his stories to you and Whitey gives him something to look forward to every day. It's a lot better than him sitting and watching that television junk for hours at a time."

"I guess that's what he'll be doing again when we go back to school."

"Probably. But, at least he's had a few weeks enjoying himself with you boys," Julia said.

"You know what, Mom?" John asked.

"What's that, John?"

"I really enjoy spending time with him. And, so does Whitey."

"That's good. I'm glad."

Whitey and John were sitting on the lawn outside of the library, looking across the street at City Hall. "It's kinda high. Do you think we can get up there?" Whitey asked.

"If you get on my shoulders, I think you'll be able to reach it and pull it down."

"What if we get caught?" Whitey asked John.

"We'll just say we were goofing around. No big deal."

"Yeah, I guess. Unless it's that cop Drollstrom. He's a mean one."

"We'll just wait until we see him drive away in his squad before we try it," John said.

"If we're gonna wait until it's dark, he should be off his shift," Whitey said. He stared at the building. "Are you sure that window is open a little bit? You must have eyes like Superman, because I can't see that," Whitey declared.

"How about we go get some binoculars?" John asked, joking.

"Hold up a minute," Whitey said, as he stood up, checked the traffic and ran across James Street to the side of the building. He stood on the sidewalk and stared up at the second story window. He turned and looked at John, gave him a thumbs up, and ran back across the street.

"Well?" John asked.

Whitey grinned. "You were right. It's open a few inches."

"So, we gonna do this?" John asked.

"Damn right, we are," Whitey replied, as he lit up a cigarette. "I'm gonna find out one way or the other if there's a tunnel under this damn street."

At nine o'clock that night, Whitey and John were standing under the fire escape, which was attached to the side of City Hall. Whitey was standing on John's shoulders, reaching for the pull down ladder. "A little more," Whitey whispered.

"Grab it," John whispered back. "I can't. . ."

"Got it," Whitey said, as he pulled the ladder down and jumped off of his friend's shoulders.

The ladder clanked as it hit the sidewalk. "Quiet," John murmured.

"You go first," Whitey told John.

"No, I think you should go first. You're lighter than I am."

Whitey gave him a confused look. "What does that have to do with it?"

John shrugged. "I don't know. I just want to be sure it's gonna hold us, I guess."

"It's a fire escape," Whitey uttered. "Of course, it's gonna hold us."

John grabbed onto the fire escape and climbed up. When he reached the window, he gently pushed the it all the way up and crawled inside. He stuck his head out the window and motioned for Whitey to come up. He turned and looked into the room, which was partially lit up by the street lights from outside. "Wow!" he said, softly.

Whitey climbed into the room and stared. "Wow!"

The two boys were looking at an auditorium, complete with a stage and hundreds of seats.

"Did you know. . ."

"Not a clue," Whitey interrupted. "What is this, anyway?"

"It looks like a theater or something like that," John said. "Gramps would know. Let's ask him tomorrow."

"And, admit we snuck in here?" Whitey asked.

"He won't say anything," John said.

"I think we should wait," Whitey told him.

"Why?"

"Maybe, he'll bring it up in one of his stories and, then, no one will know we broke in here."

John shrugged. "I guess. This is really something, isn't it?"

"Why is this room a secret? Did something horrible happen here and no one talks about it?"

"I've never heard anything about it. Let's go up on the stage."

"This is spooky. How about we get the hell out of here instead?" Whitey said. "Where's the door that goes downstairs?"

"It should be over that way," John said. "Be careful you don't make any noise."

The two boys, tiptoed across the floor and opened a door that led down to the first floor. "Be quiet," Whitey said.

They started down the stairs, trying to be as quiet as possible, but the old steps creaked beneath their weight. "Shh," John whispered every few steps.

"You shh," Whitey finally whispered back.

"Quiet," John instructed, as he stepped off the last step and reached for the door that led to the hallway on the first floor. He turned the handle. "Shit," he muttered.

"What?" Whitey asked.

"It's locked."

"Crap. Now what?"

"I guess we go back up and out the window," John told him.

"Try it again," Whitey said. "Maybe it's just stuck."

John turned the handle and pushed. "Nothing," he said.

"Let me try," Whitey said, pushing John out of the way. He grabbed the handle, turned it, and pushed. "It's locked," he said.

John stared at him. "Really?" he said, sarcastically.

"I tell you, Augie, I hear something," a woman's voice said from the other side of the door.

The two boys froze, afraid to move.

"Do we have the key for that door?" a man's voice asked.

"No. It's in the mayor's office," the woman said.

"Well, he's gone for the day. I'll check it out tomorrow, Jacquie, but there's no way anyone is up there."

"Fine," the woman said. "But, I know I heard something."

John and Whitey did not move, barely breathing in fear of being caught. Then, they turned and very slowly walked back up the stairs into the auditorium. Whitey sat down in one of the seats. "That was close. We'd be dead meat by now if Chief Austin had a key to that door." He looked around the room. "It's really dark in here," he stated.

"Go over by the windows. It's a little brighter over there."

"We have to go back down the fire escape, you know," Whitey said.

"I know. Let's just wait a few more minutes,"

John replied.

"I don't like heights," Whitey declared.

"Don't you think you should have thought about that before we climbed up here?" John said, starting to laugh.

"Shh," Whitey said. "They'll hear you."

"So, what," John said, still laughing. "They can't get up here. They don't have a key."

Whitey started to laugh. "You're right, they don't have a key," he said. He stopped laughing and grabbed John's arm. "But, they can always climb up the fire escape."

John stopped laughing and looked at him. "Crap. Let's get out of here. Now!"

The fire escape ladder clanked as it hit the sidewalk. Whitey hit the ground first, with John right on his tail. The two boys took off, running across James Street and towards the high school. They made it to the Methodist Church before Whitey tripped and went rolling onto the lawn. "Wait," he shouted.

John turned and laughed. He walked back to where Whitey was lying and fell down on the ground next to him. "That was close," he declared. "We almost got caught."

Whitey, rolled over on his back, laughing. "It's a good thing the key is in the mayor's office," he said.

"What do you think Austin would have done, if he had caught us?" John asked Whitey.

"Probably called our parents," Whitey said.

"Nah. I don't think so. I think he would have given us a talking to, and let us go."

"And, then called our parents," Whitey stated.

"Whatever. I know I'm never going up that fire escape again."

"Shit!" Whitey said. "We left that window open. Now, Austin's going to know for sure that someone was up there."

"So what? It's no big deal. He can't know it was us," John uttered. He stood up and glanced down at his friend. "Do you wanna go get a root beer?"

"I think I should head home. What about you?"

"That's probably best," John answered.

The two boys started walking home. "If your grandpa isn't feeling any better tomorrow, do you want to see if we can get into the basement?" Whitey asked John.

Fourteen

"Don't stay too long, now," Julia told the boys, as they settled in on the floor. She glanced over at Samuel. "Remember what the doctor said. You need to rest."

"I'm fine," Samuel said. He looked at the boys and smiled. "I don't know what is in that stuff the doctor gave me, but I feel a lot better."

"That's good," John said.

"Are you gonna tell us what happened to Rose?" Whitey asked.

Samuel glanced over a Julia, who was standing in the doorway. "Are you joining us today," he asked her, smiling.

Julia grinned. "Perhaps, for a little while. If it's okay with you, that is. Just like Whitey, I'd like to know what happened to Rose, too."

"It's fine with me," Samuel told her. "Boys?"

"I guess," Whitey said.

"You can't interrupt," John said. "Gramps doesn't like to be interrupted."

Samuel chuckled. "You two do enough of it. If you have any questions, Julia, feel free to ask them."

"I won't stay long," Julia said. "And, I promise I'll be quiet."

Samuel sat back, picked up a pipe, and fondled it.

"Are you smoking?" John asked, a surprised look on his face.

"No, no." Samuel told him. "I just like to hold it. I found it in the back of one of my dresser drawers. I seem to think better when I hold it."

He cleared his throat and continued the story. "Everything was pretty quiet here for the next few years," he began. "Times were tough for a lot of people, with the depression and all, but most managed to keep their heads above water."

"Now, Pearl, who, by the way, had a Creole background, not black like people thought, had married Chief Worthers and they seemed happy."

"A what background?" Whitey asked.

Julia made a slight coughing sound. "I thought we didn't interrupt," she commented.

"It's okay. How else are these idiots gonna learn?" Samuel told her, grinning. "Creole. They are people who were born in Louisiana, mostly with French and Spanish blood. It varies, I guess, but that's what I think they are. Does that sound right to you, Julia?"

"I think so," she answered. "It's a wide spread term, but that about covers it. I suggest you boys make a trip to the library some time and look it up for yourselves."

Samuel smiled at her and continued. "Ada Mae had gone back down south to Mississippi to be with her family. And, the other two girls, Azelea and Charlotte, seemed content to continue to work for Rose in the Tea Shop and live in Rose's big house."

"Buck spent about half his time here and half in Chicago. I still don't know what he did there, although, gossip was that he was part owner in a bar. Prohibition was over by now and selling liquor was no longer illegal. This, of course, cut into the Rose's profits, as her customers no longer had to pay exorbitant prices for a drink. She kept the poker games going, though, and, between the income from the Tea House and the house's cut on the games, she continued to do quite well for herself. Chief Worthers didn't push for a bigger split and settled for whatever money came his way. All in all, I'd say things were going okay."

"Well, they were until the so called ghost returned to that house. Maybe, return is the wrong word. Maybe, she was there all the time. But, something woke that ghost up and she decided to make herself known."

"What did she do?" Julia blurted out, making everyone laugh.

"Rules, Mom," John said.

"Sorry. Please, continue," she said to Samuel.

"Well, there are definitely different versions about what happened. The way I heard it is that Rose was in the kitchen when she heard a noise coming from the basement. Knowing that she was alone in the house, she was hesitant to go down there to investigate. She did, however, open the door that led to the basement and looked down the steps. Suddenly, she felt a gust of wind on her face and the kitchen door slammed shut. She tried to open the door to get back into the kitchen, but the door was stuck shut. Now, Rose was a pretty cool lady and not much could get to her, but this really scared her. She tried the door again, and it opened right away. Her legs were a little shaky and she decided she best sit down and try to calm her nerves. She pulled a chair away from the table and, just as she started to sit, the chair pulled away, and she landed right on her butt. She looked behind her, but no one was there. Stunned and scared, she stayed on the floor for a few seconds, then, stood up, gathered up her skirts, and made a mad dash for the front door."

"Wow," Julia whispered.

Samuel and the two boys smiled, but stayed quiet.

"Then, what?" Julia asked.

"She sat on the front porch until Buck showed up. She told him what had happened, but he just laughed and told her that her imagination was working overtime.

"I'm telling you, it's for real. I heard stories about a ghost being in this house, Buck. I thought it was hogwash, but, after today, I think there's one down there in that basement. So, don't you be making fun of me," Rose said, raising her voice.

"Who is it, then?" Buck asked her. "Does your ghost have a name?"

"How should I know," Rose told him. "But, I heard that there was a gypsy lady who lived here and that a ghost killed her husband."

Buck grinned. "I've heard those stories. And, she was a fortune teller not a gypsy. Besides, Rose, ghosts don't go around sticking swords in people."

"Well, a jury believed that they do. They found her innocent of killing that man."

"She was guilty as sin and she got away with murder. Believe me, there are no ghosts living here."

104

If you don't believe in ghosts and you're so brave, why don't you sleep in the basement tonight?" Rose asked him.

"Well, I would, but there aren't any beds down there," Buck said, grinning.

"There's an old cot stored down there. You can sleep on that," Rose told him.

"I'm not sleeping on any old cot and certainly not in the basement."

"Are you afraid? You are, aren't you?" Rose asked.

"This is ridiculous. I'm not sleeping in the basement. That's final and I don't want to hear anything more about it."

"Fine. But, I'm not staying here tonight. I'm going to get a room at the Tremont."

"Rose, you're being silly. I'll be here for the next few days. I'll make sure you're safe."

"I'll be safe, all right," she said. *"Because, I'll be at the Tremont."*

"Isn't there a poker game here tonight?" Buck asked. *"You need to be here for that."*

Rose gave him a dirty look. "You handle it. I'm going to the hotel."

She turned and started to leave the room, obviously still upset and frightened.

"Rose, wait," Buck called to her.

She turned and looked at him. "What?"

"Before you go storming out of here, there's something we need to talk about."

"It can wait. I'm leaving."

"Please, sit down for a few minutes. This is

important."

She stared at him, curious at what he had to tell her. Finally, she sat down and sighed. "What's so important?"

"I'm getting married," Buck blurted out.

Rose sat back in her chair, obviously surprised by Buck's statement. "To whom? I didn't even know you were seeing someone."

"It's a lady from Chicago. We've been seeing each other for almost a year now."

"But, you've never said anything. If you're so serious about this woman, how come I've never met her?"

Buck looked away. "I wasn't planning. . . I mean, I had no intentions of. . ." He turned away from his sister and took a deep breath. "She's going to have my baby. I've rented a nice apartment in Chicago for us, and we're going to be married next week."

Rose kept quiet, trying to absorb Buck's news.

"I'm sorry I didn't say anything before," he said. "I didn't mean for this to happen, but seeing as how it did, I need to step up and take responsibility."

"Do you love her?" Rose asked him."

Buck hesitated. "I do," he finally said. "I think we can have a good life together."

Rose smiled. "Well, then, I'm happy for you. When will I get to meet. . ." She looked up at her brother. "I don't even know her name."

"It's Belle."

"Belle," Rose repeated. "So, when do I get to meet Belle?"

"There's something else, Rose," he said, looking

106

away.

 Rose didn't respond, waiting for him to continue

 "I'll be staying in Chicago from now on. I won't be coming back here to help out anymore. My business is going really well, and I'm needed there full time. You understand, don't you?"

 Rose stood up and faced him. "So, this is it, then? After all these years that we've worked together and everything I've done for you, this is how you tell me you're finished? Shame on you, Buck. I deserve better than this from you."

 "I'm sorry, Rose," he told her.

 "Bullshit," she shouted. She took a couple of steps towards him, raised her hand, and slapped him hard across his face. "Bullshit!" she yelled again, then, turned and ran out of the room.

 "Rose," Buck yelled, as he started to follow her. "Stop. I'm sorry."

 Suddenly, Buck felt something strike him hard in the abdomen. He grunted and glanced down at his stomach, shocked to see his shirt covered with blood. As his knees buckled and he went down, he felt a rush of cold air pass over him. "Rose," he cried out, "help me."

 Rose didn't hear him call out to her, as she shut the front door and headed to the hotel.

 Julia stared at Samuel, not saying anything. She looked at her son and Whitey, who were totally absorbed in the story, and understood why they came back day after day to listen to the old man. "I've got to start dinner," she said, as she stood up and headed for

107

the door.

"Don't you want to find out what happened next?" John asked her.

"Well. . ." she hesitated. "I do, but I should get dinner started. Your dad will be home soon."

"Fix him a sandwich," Samuel said. "He doesn't need a big meal every day."

Julia looked at Samuel and smiled. "I guess a sandwich today would be okay." She sat back down and waited for him to continue.

"Go on, Gramps," John said.

"Azalea and Charlotte found Buck a few hours later. Charlotte called the doctor, who asked her to check for a pulse, which she did. After a few moments, she told the doctor that she couldn't find one and there was no need for him to rush over. Then, she called Chief Worthers and told him that Buck was dead and he should come right away. When Worthers asked to speak to Rose, Charlotte informed him that she wasn't there and didn't know where she was."

"Worthers arrived in his squad car, sirens blaring, and lights flashing. Azelea and Charlotte met him at the door, tears running down their cheeks, obviously distraught over the death of their friend. Worthers asked where the body was, and they pointed to the doorway between the kitchen and dining room. He took one look at Buck, who was lying in a pool of blood, and agreed that he was – indeed - dead."

"A few moments later, the doctor came strolling up the steps and into the house. He went over to where Worthers and the girls were standing and looked down at Buck. Very gingerly, he knelt down and checked to see if Buck had a pulse. He looked up at Worthers and frowned. Then, he bent over Buck's body to see if he could feel Buck's breath against his cheek. Suddenly, the doctor straightened up and yelled at Worthers to call for an ambulance."

"He was alive?" Julia asked.

"He certainly was. But, Buck had lost a lot of blood, his wound was serious, and no one thought he would make it. Emergency surgery was done, and, due to so much blood loss, the doctor gave him a fifty-fifty chance of making it."

"While the doctor was performing Buck's surgery, Worthers questioned the two ladies regarding Rose's whereabouts, but, once again, he was told that they had no idea where she might be. He informed Azelea and Charlotte that the house was a crime scene and they needed to make arrangements to spend the night elsewhere. Charlotte immediately called Pearl, and when she told her the situation, Pearl said they should come stay with her. Worthers assigned a rookie cop to keep an eye on Rose's house, and told him to let him know the minute she was back home."

"After Worthers placed some saw horses to block off the entrances to Rose's house, he headed to the hospital. He was determined to get a statement out of Buck the minute he woke up – if, he woke up."

"Wait," John said. "Did you say saw horses?"

"That's what they used back then, John. Not yellow tape. I'm not even sure if it had been invented in 1935. So, they used saw horses that had been painted yellow."

"Oh," John said. "Okay."

"Well, Worthers fell asleep in a chair outside the surgical area of the hospital and missed seeing Buck being wheeled into a recovery room. In fact, it wasn't until a few hours later that the sound of carts, being pushed through the hallway, woke him. Breakfast was being served."

"And, I hate to interrupt," Julia said. "But, I really need to get dinner ready. Isaac will be home any minute now."

"Then, I'll stop for now," Samuel said, clearing his throat. "I need a break, anyway."

"Ah," Whitey moaned. "Just when the story was getting really good."

Fifteen

"It's not this one, either," John whispered, as he closed the door. "There are just cleaning supplies in here."

"That just leaves the one down there," Whitey told him, as he pointed to a door.

"Nah, that's not it," John said, quietly. "That's the door that leads up to the theater."

"You boys looking for something?" a voice asked.

"Whoa!" Whitey said, startled. He turned and saw Chief Austin standing behind him, looking very serious.

"Whitey. John." Austin said, acknowledging them. "Is there something I can do for you two?"

"Nope," John replied, his face turning bright red. "We just came in to use the can."

"Well, I sure hope you don't plan on peeing in there," Austin said, trying to keep a straight face.

"No, we weren't going to. . . We just wondered where that door went, that's all," John said.

"It's none of your business, boys. And, that door is supposed to be locked." He stared at the two boys, who hadn't moved. "Well? Are you two going to stand there all day?"

"No, Sir," John said. "Come on, Whitey, let's go."

As they started to leave the building, Whitey turned back and looked at Chief Austin.

"Something else?" Austin asked him.

"I was just wondering which door leads to the basement," Whitey said.

John grabbed Whitey's arm and started to pull

him towards the exit. "What's wrong with you?" he muttered.

"Wait a minute," Austin called out. "Why do you want to know that?"

"Well, I'm interested in architect and design and this is a great old building and I'm just wondering where everything is, that's all," Whitey said, convincingly. "I'm trying to decide what I want to do when I graduate and I'm thinking about being an architect."

"Is that right?" Austin asked, wondering if Whitey was pulling his leg.

"Yes, Sir. There are a lot of interesting buildings in Columbus, just like this one."

"I guess," Austin said. "Well, you boys run along. I've got work to do."

"So, where is it?" Whitey asked.

"What is what?" Austin replied, not sure what he was referring to.

"The door to the basement. I can't figure out where it is."

Chief Austin stared at Whitey for a moment. "If you are really interested in where the door to the basement is, I suggest you and your friend make a trip to the library. I believe there are copies of the blueprints for most of the older buildings in Columbus there," he told him. "Now get out of here and let me get back to work."

"Good idea. Thanks, Chief," Whitey said. He looked at John and grinned. "Let's go."

Just as they started down the steps to exit the building, Chief Austin called out for them to wait a minute. "Shit," John whispered, as he turned around.

Austin studied the two boys for a couple of seconds. "You two know anything about how that window upstairs got opened up?"

"Not me," Whitey and John both shouted, turned, and ran out of the building.

Chief Austin grinned. "Like hell they don't," he muttered to himself.

As John and Whitey came through the back door into the kitchen, John let the screen door slam shut. His mother looked at him and frowned. "How many times must I ask you to hold that door so it doesn't slam?"

"Sorry. Do you have a cake in the oven?"

"No, but that doesn't mean you can let the door slam shut."

"Is Gramps awake?"

Julia smiled. "He is. He was asking about you boys."

Whitey smiled. "Does he feel like talking?"

"Well, Whitey, he just might. Why don't you go ask him?" she answered.

Grinning from ear to ear, Whitey headed for Samuel's bedroom. "Come on, Poop. What are you waiting for?"

Samuel took the pipe out of his mouth and laid it on the small table next to his chair. "So, what have you boys been up to?" he asked John and Whitey.

"Nothing," Whitey told him.

"We've just been waiting for you to wake up and

tell us more about Buck and Rose," John said.

Samuel sat back in his chair, closed his eyes for a moment, and began. "After Chief Worthers woke up, he tracked down the doctor who had done Buck's surgery and asked for the bullet."

"There's no bullet," the doctor told him. "Buck wasn't shot."

"What happened, then? Was he stabbed?"

"No, he wasn't stabbed, either. It's really a strange phenomenal. I've heard about cases like this, but I never thought I'd see one with my own eyes."

"I should have believed her," Worthers muttered.

"I'm sorry," Dr. Poszert said. "I didn't get that."

"Rose told me that she had a ghost in her house, but I didn't pay any attention to her. I figure the same ghost that murdered that guy that swallowed swords probably did this to Buck. Do you remember that, doctor?"

Dr. Poszert started to laugh. "A ghost didn't do this to Buck, you idiot," he said. "He had his appendix removed a few months ago, and the incision opened up. It's rare, but it happens. Sometimes the wound gets infected, or the stitches don't hold, and it will break open. It must hurt like hell when it happens. Anyway, there was a vein that popped when the incision opened, causing the extreme blood loss." He shook his head, grinning. "I can't believe a grown man like you would believe there are such things as ghosts. And, you a policeman, on top of it."

"So, you're saying it was a freak accident," Worthers stated.

"It was. There's no one to blame here, Chief."

Chief Worthers, now red in the face from embarrassment, turned and started to walk away. After a few steps, he turned and yelled, "Don't call me an idiot."

"Buck eventually recovered," Samuel said. "He was in the hospital for about a week. Rose, Azelea, and Charlotte took care of him for another ten days or so. Then, one day he hopped the train to Chicago, and that was the last anyone saw of him."

"So, there wasn't a ghost?" Julia asked.

"Maybe. Maybe not." Samuel replied. "Not long after that Rose sold the Tea House to Azelea and Charlotte. Between them, they had saved enough money to buy her out and to buy a small house on Spring Street. They packed up their belongings and moved to their new house a few months after Buck had gone back to Chicago"

"Rose was now all alone in that big house and, from what I heard, she fell into a deep depression. She stopped hosting those poker games, and, after that, she pretty much became a recluse. She had her groceries delivered every few weeks with instructions that the delivery boy should ring the bell and leave the groceries by the door. There was always an envelope with money waiting for him. This went on for almost a year, and, then, one day the grocery orders stopped. McNulty, who owned the grocery store, finally talked to Chief Worthers and told him that Rose wasn't ordering groceries anymore. He wondered if Worthers thought someone should check on her."

"After thinking about it for a few hours, Worthers took McNulty's advice and drove over to see Rose. She didn't answer the door, so he broke the window, reached in, and undid the lock. The house was cold and dark, and stunk to high heaven. He called out Rose's name a few times, but he already knew she wouldn't answer."

"She was dead, wasn't she?" John murmured.

"She was," Samuel told him. "Worthers found her in the front foyer. At first glance, he thought she looked beautiful lying there in her white lace robe. But, when he got a little closer, it wasn't a pretty sight he was looking at and the stench was overbearing. He took one look at her rotting face and ran out of the house and vomited onto the bushes. Remember, Rose had been a beautiful woman, but the sight that Worthers saw that day haunted him for the rest of his life."

Samuel paused, took a sip of water, and picked up his pipe. He brushed a tear from his eye, and smiled. "Sorry. I guess I always had special feelings for Rose and this makes me kind of sad."

"Why don't we stop for today," Julia suggested.

"No!" John and Whitey exclaimed at the same time.

"I think I can go a little longer," Samuel told her.

"If you feel you're up to it," Julia said.

"I do." He took a deep breath, coughed a little, and continued. "Rose was buried a few days after her autopsy. The doctor said her heart was bad, and that was probably the cause of her death. Of course, the word on the street was that she died from fright."

116

"Can you die from being scared?" John interrupted.

"I guess you can, if you're so scared that your heart explodes," Samuel replied.

"I guess that's what they must mean when they say somebody was scared to death," Whitey added.

"Anyway," Samuel continued, "the turnout at her funeral might have been the biggest ever. If you two are ever up by the cemetery, you should take a look at her headstone. It's probably one of the largest stones up there."

"Her brother, Buck, who was her only living relative, put the house up for sale and went back to Chicago to be with his wife and little boy. Azelea and Charlotte tried to make a go of their tea house business, but with the depression and money being so tight, they finally closed the doors. The last I heard, they had sold their house and moved back down south somewhere near Ida Mae."

"What about Pearl?" Julia asked.

"Ah, yes. Pearl. She had a good life with Chief Worthers for around ten years or so. He suddenly died of a massive heart attack, leaving her alone to care for their three children. She had folks in New York, so she eventually packed up everything and moved there, to be closer to them."

"Wow," Julia said. "That's quite a story, Grandpa. That house has sure seen its share of weirdness."

"That, it has," Samuel agreed. "It's strange, but all the while I worked there that house had a different kind of feel to it than other houses I worked on. I know that doesn't make much sense, but a lot of us guys hated working there. Maybe, it's because so many of us got hurt on the job. I can't explain it, really. Sometimes, I think that house might have been cursed."

"Grandpa?" Julia hesitated, thinking about what she wanted to say.

"What is it?" Samuel asked.

"Well, I'm trying to get it right, but wasn't there a house on that property before the one that's there now?"

"Yeah. It's the small house between that one and the lumber company. We moved that little house back to make room for the big one. When Von Schmidt bought the property, there was a woman renter who lived in that little house. Well, the seller made a stipulation that Von Schmidt had to move the house to the back lot and give it to her or he wouldn't sell the property. Von Schmidt reluctantly agreed, even though it meant losing a large portion of his yard."

"Isn't it hard to move a house? I mean, do you have to take it all apart and then put it back together again?" John inquired.

"It's a big job, but I've seen bigger houses than that being moved. Moving that house wasn't that big a deal, as we only had to move it a few feet, and it wasn't that large," Samuel told him.

"Well, I guess I better get supper ready," Julia stated. She stood up and walked over to Samuel. "Thank you," she said, as she bent down and kissed him on the cheek. "You tell one heck of a good story."

"Yeah, Gramps," John agreed. "This is

interesting. Who knew so much shit. . ."

"Language, John," Julia said, as she walked out of the room.

"I mean, who knew so much crap could go on in one house," he said, grinning.

"Did Rose's brother ever sell the house?" Whitey asked.

John looked at him. "No, it's still for sale, you dummy."

"Up yours, Poop." Whitey stood up and stretched. "Guess I better get home. Thanks for the story, Mr. H. Can't wait to hear what's next. Same time tomorrow morning?"

"If I'm still breathing," Samuel told him.

Sixteen

"Finish your cereal, John."

John shoveled the last few spoonsful of his corn flakes into his mouth. "Done," he cried out, as he pushed his chair back from the table, and headed towards Samuel's room.

"Dish, please," Julia called out.

John sighed, as he turned around, picked up the dish, and handed it to his mother.

"Thank you," she said, smiling.

He hurried into the old man's room, and sat down on the floor. "Okay, you can start now," he told Samuel.

"About time," Whitey muttered.

"Hey, it's not my fault that. . ."

"Enough, boys," Samuel interrupted.

"Sorry," John said.

"Me, too," Whitey piped in.

Samuel drank the last of his coffee and put the cup down. "Let's see, now. I've told you most of the interesting things that happened in that house. There's not much left to tell you."

Whitey, obviously getting upset, stared at him. "Well, I think you're forgetting something," he muttered.

Samuel looked at him and shrugged. "I am? Well, a few more little things happened there, but what I've told you so far, pretty much covers it."

"What about. . . I know you said I shouldn't ask again. . . Never mind. Forget I said anything."

"Oh, you mean the tunnel, right?"

"Right," Whitey agreed.

"Gotcha," Samuel said, laughing.

Whitey grinned. "Is there one there or not?"

"I'm getting to it. Just let me finish up about the history of that house. Deal?"

"Deal," Whitey agreed.

"Actually, there really isn't that much more to tell. It was probably 1944 or so before that house was sold again. Buck hadn't bothered to pay the taxes for years, and, eventually, a tax lien was put on the property. An investor picked it up dirt cheap and rented it out. It was like that house had a revolving door; the way renters came and went. I don't think anyone stayed in that house longer than six months. A few families even packed up in the middle of the night and took off. There was some talk again about the house being haunted but no one paid it any mind. Eventually, the owner got tired of the hassle of dealing with fly by night renters, and he put the house on the market."

"No one wanted it. A For Sale sign sat on the front lawn for months. The investor lowered the price a few times, and, finally, an elderly couple purchased it. Hatcher was their name, I believe. Yes, it was Hatcher. Chester and Mary Hatcher. Anyway, it seemed strange that an older couple wanted such a big house, until the word got out that they intended to foster children. Before you knew it, the house was overrun with kids of all ages. Those that were old enough went to the public school, but most of those kids were just little tots waiting to be adopted or taken in by some family."

"The foster parents were compensated well

121

enough, but the state had strict rules that had to be adhered to. Eventually, the Hatchers got greedy, spending less on the kids and putting more in their pockets for themselves. They got caught and that was the end of their fostering. They stayed in the house for another year or so." Samuel thought for a few moments. "You know, I don't know what happened to them. I guess I was out of the loop by then."

"We were born by then," John commented. "Whitey and I would have been about six back in 1945."

"I remember," Samuel said. "You were such cute little boys. What happened?"

"Funny, Gramps," John said, laughing. "We're still cute. Right, Whitey?"

"I am, but you're as ugly as a toad with warts," Whitey responded, grinning.

"You're both ugly," the old man said. "Anyway, that's about it. The Pearys bought the house in 1950 and have lived there ever since. As far as I know, they haven't been visited by any ghosts, and no one has died or been murdered there. Of course, that's not saying that it won't happen."

"Well, Mrs. Peary did disappear," John said.

"No, she didn't. She walked away under her own free will," Samuel said, correcting him.

"But, Sarah said she hasn't heard from her mother since she left."

"Doesn't mean she disappeared, John. I know for a fact that she went out west to stay with one of her sisters for a while."

"Where is she now?" John asked him.

"I have no idea. Have you asked that Peary girl out on a date yet?" Samuel asked John, changing the subject.

"Poop loves her," Whitey teased.

"Knock it off, Whitey," John demanded. He looked up at the old man and grinned. "I'm waiting until school starts. I'll probably ask her to a dance or something."

"Well, don't wait too long. Someone else may ask her out first and you don't want to let her get away," Samuel told him.

John shrugged. "I guess."

"So, are you gonna tell us about the tunnel now?" Whitey asked.

"Not now. I have an appointment in half an hour. I guess we can finish this up tomorrow."

"Whaat?" Whitey moaned.

Julia stuck her head in the door and looked at Samuel. "We have to leave in a few minutes, Grandpa. Do you need to use the bathroom before we go?"

"I'm fine, Julia. Just give me a minute."

"Where are you going?" John asked.

"You don't need to know that," Julia snapped.

John looked surprised at her bluntness. "I'm sorry I asked. I didn't know it was a big secret."

Using his cane, Samuel slowly stood up and stretched. "I'm really stiff this morning. Too much sitting around, I guess."

"So, I'll see you tomorrow?" Whitey asked.

"Yep," Samuel said. "I'll have John let you know what time."

Whitey stood up, walked over the Samuel and

hugged him. Samuel looked questioningly over Whitey's shoulder at John, who shrugged, indicating that he had no idea what was going on. Whitey let go and backed away from the old man.

"What was that for?" Samuel said, obviously unnerved by the show of affection.

"I just want you to know that I've really enjoyed spending time with you," Whitey told him, turning a little red in the face.

"Thank you, Whitey. I've enjoyed spending time with you, too," he declared.

"Maybe, after school starts and if we have enough time, you could tell us about some of the other stuff that went on around here back in the old days."

Samuel wiped his eye with the back of his hand. "I'd like that," he said. "Now, Julia is waiting for me. I've got to get going."

John watched the old man walk out of the room. He turned and looked at Whitey. "What the hell, Whitey. What was that all about?"

"What can I say, Poop? I love that old guy."

Seventeen

"Mornin'," Whitey mumbled, as he sat down next to John.

"Morning, Whitey," Julia said, smiling. "How are you this morning?"

"Tired. You got any coffee left?" he asked Julia.

"When did you start drinking coffee?" John asked.

"Today," Whitey said, raising his voice. "Is that okay with you?"

"Hey, don't yell at me just because you're tired. It's not my fault you stayed up late watching Steve Allen."

Samuel, holding his coffee cup, walked into the kitchen. He sat down at the table and pushed the cup towards Julia. "Coffee, please."

"Me, too," Whitey said.

Julia smiled, reached for the coffee pot and poured the remainder of the coffee into Samuel's cup. "That's the end of the coffee," she said. "Looks like you're out of luck, Whitey."

"Do you have any orange juice?" he asked.

"Will you get that, John?" Julia asked, hearing the front doorbell ring.

"Are you expecting someone?" Samuel asked her.

"No, I'm not," she replied, holding back a smile.

"Mom, it's the police." John yelled. "Chief Austin wants to talk to you."

"Well, tell him to come in," she said, loudly.

"I'm in," Austin said, as he walked into the

kitchen.

Julia looked at Austin and smiled. "Well, good morning, Augie. What brings you here?"

Augie looked around the kitchen. "I'm glad you're here, Whitey. It saves me a trip to your house."

"What for?" Whitey asked, starting to turn red in the face.

"I'm sorry, Julia, but I need to take John and Whitey down to the station," Austin said, ignoring Whitey's question.

"What in the world for?" she asked. "Are they in trouble?"

"I'm not sure. I have some questions for them, and it would be easier to do it down at the station."

Julia looked at John, her hands on her hips, and sighed. "You better not have done anything stupid, young man, or your father will see to you."

Whitey snickered and turned away.

"What's so funny, Whitey?" she asked, waiting for an answer. "Well?" she persisted when he didn't answer her.

"Sorry," Whitey said. "It just sounded funny when you called him a young man."

"Well, I'd say that by the serious look on Chief Austin's face, that there's nothing to laugh about. Am I right, Chief Austin?"

"Well, now, let's not get ahead of ourselves. I'm not sure they did anything wrong, Julia. That's why I want to talk to them."

"They're minors. I'm coming with you," Samuel declared.

"Sam, I don't know if that's necessary. I just

126

want to ask them a few questions. I certainly don't want to put you out by having you come down to the station and all."

"Well, necessary or not, I'm coming. Is your squad out front?"

"Yes, but. . ."

"Then, you can give me a ride," he informed Austin. He stood up, grabbed his cane, and headed towards the front door. "Come on, boys. Let's go"

John looked at his mother. "Mom, do we have to go?"

"I think it best if you do. Just mind your manners."

"Yes, ma'am," John said.

"You, too, Whitey," she said, as she turned away from them so they wouldn't see her smiling.

Austin opened the back door of the squad car so the two boys could get in. He helped Samuel get into the passenger seat, walked around the car, got in and started it.

Whitey poked John in the ribs to get his attention. "Do you know what's going on?" he mouthed.

John shook his head no.

"Do you think they know it was us that left the window open?" Whitey whispered.

"No talking back there," Austin told them.

"It sure is a beautiful day, isn't it?" Samuel asked, making small talk.

"It sure is. I can't believe that summer's almost over," Austin remarked.

"It sure went fast," Samuel said. "School starts next week."

"Yep," Austin said. "Sure does.

Austin waited for a car to pass by, then, made a left handed turn on Dickason, pulled up in front of City Hall, and parked the squad car. "Hold up a minute, Sam, and I'll help you out."

"I appreciate that," Samuel said.

Austin walked around the car and helped the old man get out. Then, he opened the back door and motioned for the two boys to exit the vehicle. "All right, everyone," he said, "let's go and get comfortable."

Chief Austin showed them to a small room with a table and a few chairs, and asked them to get comfortable. "I need to get another chair," he stated, as he walked out of the room and closed the door.

John looked at Samuel. "What's going on, Gramps?" he asked.

Samuel looked over at him and shrugged. "I haven't a clue," he told John. "Did you boys do something wrong?"

"Not me," Whitey said, emphatically.

"John?"

"What?" John replied.

"Are you in trouble for some reason?"

"I don't think so," John said, looking away.

The door opened and Chief Austin walked in carrying a folding chair. He opened the chair, pushed it closer to the table, and sat down. "First of all, I want you two to know that you are not in trouble."

Whitey looked over at John and grinned. "I knew

it, 'cause we didn't do anything wrong," he said. "But, why are we here?" he asked Austin.

"You want to tell them, Sam?" Austin asked.

"Nah. You go ahead," Samuel said, as he sat back in his chair and stared the Whitey and John.

"Okay. Your grandfather, who is sitting over there looking so proud of himself. . ."

"Great-grandfather," Samuel interrupted. "I'm his great-grandfather."

Austin smiled. "I stand corrected," he declared. "Let me start over. Your great-grandfather stopped by yesterday and asked me for a favor. Under different circumstances, I would have said no. But, I've known Sam for a long time and he's done a lot for this town and I figure this town owes him one. He asked me if I would show you boys the basement of this building."

"What?" Whitey said, obviously surprised. He turned and looked at John. "Did you know about this, Poop?"

John shook his head no. "Gramps? You did this?"

"Let the man talk, boys," Samuel said, grinning from ear to ear.

"It didn't make a lot of sense to me when you boys were here the other day, looking around and asking about the door to the basement," Austin continued. "Then, Sam told me that while he was telling you boys about Columbus, the rumor about the tunnels came up. Well, then, I knew what you were up to. I figured it would be better if I showed you the basement, than have to arrest you one of these days for breaking and entering."

129

Whitey stared at Austin. "You said tunnels. Is there more than one?" He turned and looked at John. "Did you hear that? He said tunnels."

"Whoa," Austin said. "Don't get excited. Everyone knows about the tunnel at Kurth's. It's been there for years."

"What about the tunnel that goes to that house on Ludington Street?" John asked.

"I doubt that ever existed," Austin replied. "I've heard the rumors, but if there actually was one, it was filled in a long time ago. There are some others that ran from store to store, but those are probably gone, too. However, I don't think that the tunnel which you're so interested in ." He hesitated. "The one you think goes from here to under the War Memorial. . ." He stood up. " Well, let's go take a look, shall we?"

Chief Austin started leading the boys out of the room, then, turned and looked at Samuel. "You coming, Sam?" he asked.

"I don't think I can make the stairs, Augie," Samuel replied. "I figure I'll get down, but I won't be able to make it back up. Besides, I'd hate to make the trip and then find out it was all for nothing," he added.

Whitey looked at him and frowned. "Don't say that, Mr. H. I just know there's a tunnel down there."

"We'll see," Samuel said.

Samuel watched as Chief Austin and the boys walked away. "Damn this old body," he uttered.

Eighteen

"This way," Chief Austin instructed, as he led the boys out of the police station and into the mayor's office. "Morning," he said to the woman sitting behind a desk.

She looked up and smiled. "Morning, Chief. Are these the boys you were telling me about?"

"Sure are. This is Whitey and John. Boys, meet Pattie, the mayor's secretary

"Hello," the boys mumbled.

"Is it open?" Austin asked her.

"Sure is. Just go through that door there. I've turned the lights on, but you need to be careful going down those steps. They're pretty steep."

"Thanks, Pattie," Austin said. "Okay, boys, you heard the lady. Let's go and be careful, will you? I don't feel like making a trip to the emergency room this morning."

Austin led them through a door at the back of the room, and down the steps. They stood at the bottom of the stairs and looked around.

"It's cold down here," John declared.

"Stinks, too," Whitey said.

"It's a basement," Austin stated. "What did you expect?"

"I don't know," Whitey said. "We have a basement at our house, but it doesn't smell bad like this."

"No one ever comes down here," Austin told him. "It's been closed up for years. It's old and damp and musty smelling."

"I know," Whitey said. "I'm not complaining or anything."

"I'm glad to hear that," Austin said, "or, I'd send your ass back upstairs."

"Where is it?" John asked Austin.

"Where is what?"

"The opening to the tunnel."

Austin reached over and picked up two flashlights that were on a small table. "Here, take these," he said, as he handed a flashlight to each of the boys. "The lights are not that good down here. You're gonna need these. You've got one hour." He turned and started up the stairs.

"Wait," John called out. "Where are you going?"

Austin turned and looked at him. "I don't care if there's a tunnel down here or not. However, if you want to know, you better start looking. One hour, boys."

"What are we looking for?" Whitey asked.

"Buried treasure," John said, sarcastically.

Whitey thought for a moment. "There's not going to be an opening," he told John. "What we need to find is where there was an opening which has been sealed up. If it was cemented closed, the concrete will be a different color than the rest," he continued, getting excited now. "You take that side and I'll take this side," he directed John.

Chief Austin, who had been listening to the boys as he climbed the stairs, smiled to himself. "Don't forget to check the two back rooms," he yelled.

John looked at Whitey and frowned. "There are back rooms?"

Whitey shrugged. "How should I know?" he said. "It's pretty dark down here, Chief," Whitey called out.

Austin chuckled. "Well, you can come back up if you're scared. Or, I can ask Pattie to come down and babysit you, if you want."

"We're good," John yelled.

"One hour, boys," Austin said, as he shut the door and went to join Samuel.

Forty-five minutes later, Whitey, his face and hands covered with grime, walked into the room. "We found it," he told Samuel, smiling. "We found the opening."

Austin's head jerked up, surprise written all over his face. "You what?" he asked.

"The opening to the tunnel. We found it," Whitey repeated.

"No way," Austin said. "There's no tunnel down there."

"There sure is," John said, as he joined Whitey in the room. He held his hands up, indicating how dirty he was. "I've got to go wash my hands," he muttered. "I'll be right back."

"Me, too," Whitey said, joining John to go wash up.

Austin stared at Samuel and grinned. "You old devil. You knew all along that there was a tunnel down there, didn't you?"

"I was pretty sure," Samuel said, laughing. "You should have seen the look on your face. Too bad I didn't have a camera."

"How did you know?"

"Hell, I worked on most of the older buildings in this town at one time or the other. Von Schmidt had that tunnel added when he was Chief of Police, shortly before his wife disappeared. I wouldn't say for sure, but I'd bet you anything that's where Von Schmidt's wife ended up."

Austin looked shocked. "That's a hell of a statement, Sam," he said.

"Well, it's either there or she's buried in that cistern in that house where he used to live. I'd bet on the tunnel here, though. The workers that Von Schmidt brought to town worked here and in the basement of that house. Von Schmidt's wife was still alive when they left town, so it wouldn't have been the house." Samuel thought for a moment. "Nope, Augie, it's not the house."

"Do you seriously think there's a body in that tunnel?" Austin asked.

Samuel looked over at the doorway and frowned. "How long have you two been standing there?"

John looked away. "Nothing," he replied, nervously.

"What?" Samuel said.

"I mean, not long. We didn't hear nothing, did we, Whitey?"

"Not me," Whitey told him. He looked at Chief Austin and smiled. "Do you want us to show you where the opening is?" he said, smugly.

Austin sighed. "Damn. If I'd known they were going to find something, I wouldn't have let them go down there," he told Samuel.

"What's the big deal?" Samuel asked. "It was

134

almost fifty years ago."

"Sam, if there's the slightest chance that there is a body in that tunnel, I have to check it out," Austin said.

John turned and looked at Whitey. "Wow!" he mouthed.

"Yes, wow," Austin agreed, who had seen John. "Now, it's a matter of getting the city to pay to have that tunnel dug out again."

"It's open," John declared. "You can look right into it."

"What are you saying?" Austin asked.

"We poked a hole through the cement." John said. "It wasn't like the rest of the cement. You know, it was more like plaster of paris. We were pounding on the walls and some of it cracked, so we hit it harder, and we made a hole." He grinned. "We shined our flashlights into it, but we couldn't see much. But, I think you could probably crawl right to the end, Chief Austin."

"I'll go," Whitey volunteered.

"Like hell you will," Samuel said.

"No one is going into that hole," Austin uttered. "At least, not yet."

"What are you going to do?" Samuel asked.

"I'm not really sure," Austin said. "I think the first thing I need to do is get a construction engineer out here to check it out and see if it's safe to enter it."

"Can we be here when he checks it out?" Whitey inquired.

"No," Austin told him.

"But, we found it. If it wasn't for us you wouldn't

even know about it."

"No," Austin repeated.

"But, we should be. . ."

"No, and that is final," Austin interrupted. "Besides, it will probably be weeks before we know if it is safe enough to go in there."

"Actually, Augie, I think the boys have a point," Samuel said. "If they weren't so damn curious, we wouldn't be having this conversation."

"If they weren't so damn curious, one of the windows on the second floor wouldn't have been left wide open," Austin declared. "Right, boys?"

Whitey, looking guilty as sin, shrugged and looked away.

"What window are you talking about?" John asked, innocently.

"You gonna play stupid?"

"Augie, are the boys in trouble for something?" Samuel inquired.

Chief Austin hesitated for a moment. "Nah, I guess not."

"Good to hear," Samuel said. "I guess that's it, then. Boys, I think it's time to leave. Julia will have dinner on the table in a little while."

"You want to have dinner with us, Chief Austin?" John asked.

"I don't think I can," Austin told him. "I've wasted the morning and I've got a lot to catch up on."

"I think mom is making chicken," John declared. "She always makes a lot more than we can eat."

"It sounds tempting, but I think I'll pass. Let's go. I'll give you a ride back home."

Nineteen

"Chief Austin called this morning," Samuel casually mentioned, as he helped himself to another helping of mashed potatoes.

John glanced over at him, waiting for him to continue.

"Really? That took long enough. What did he say?" Isaac asked his grandfather.

"The engineer has completed his tests and they have the go ahead to send someone into the tunnel."

"Yes!" John shouted.

"Table manners," his father said.

"Sorry. Can I be excused?"

"You haven't finished your supper," Julia said. "Don't you want desert?"

"Later, okay. I want to call Whitey."

"You might want to wait a minute, John," Samuel told him. "I have more news."

John, who had started to get up from his chair, plopped back down and looked at Samuel. "What is it?"

"I got permission for you and Whitey to be there when they go in."

"No way," John exclaimed.

"Hold on, before you get too excited," Samuel told him. "You have to promise to stay out of the way, and keep your mouths shut. You can watch, but that's all. And, if anything goes wrong, you are to leave the building immediately. Understood?"

"Yes, sir," John said, as he again started to leave the table.

"And," Samuel continued.

John sat back down and looked at him. "Yes?"

"And, Whitey's parents need to agree to it. And, so do yours. In writing," Samuel finished.

John looked over at his father. "Dad? Is it okay?"

Isaac shrugged. "If it's okay with your mother, it's okay with me."

"Grandpa, do you know when they are doing this?" Julia asked. "I don't think John should miss school, so I'll only agree if it's on a week-end."

"Ah, Mom," John whined. "That's not fair."

"Fair or not, that's the only way you're going back down into that basement."

"Quit your bellyaching, John. It's in a couple of weeks, on November third," Samuel said. "And, it's a Saturday."

"Now, you may go call Whitey," Julia said. "And, tell him that I need to speak with his mother before you hang up."

"Thanks, Mom, but I think I'll go over to his house. I want to see the look on his face when I give him the news."

"Don't forget to tell his mother to call me," Julia told him.

"Thanks, Dad," John called out as he started to run out of the room. He hesitated, then, walked over to his great-grandfather and hugged him. "Thanks, Gramps. You're the best."

The small room in the basement, where the tunnel opening had been found, was on the south side of the building. Supposedly, the tunnel ran under

James Street and ended under the Civil War Memorial on Dickason Blvd.

John and Whitey were sitting in the room on folding chairs, with approximately twenty more people, waiting for the event to begin,

"I can't see the opening," Whitey complained. "This is dumb, Poop. Let's see if we can get closer."

"Just stay where you are," John told him. "If you get up, someone may take your chair."

"How come there are so many people here, anyway?"

"How should I know? We're just lucky that Gramps talked Chief Austin into letting us be here."

Whitey slouched down in his chair. "I guess," he said.

"He's here," a woman sitting in the front row told the lady next to her.

John and Whitey glanced over at the door to the room and saw a man enter, wearing protective clothing and a helmet. The helmet had a clear section covering the face, so the man could see out. Whitey poked John and grinned. "It's him. That's the guy that's going into the tunnel," he said, excited.

"There's Chief Austin, too," John said.

Austin walked just inside the doorway and looked over the roomful of people. "May I have your attention, please."

The room went silent, waiting for him to speak. "The man you see standing here, looking like something from outer space, is Mr. Roger Abbott. He is a civil engineer and has been working with us for the past few weeks to determine if it is safe to enter the

139

tunnel. Some of us had heard the rumors about a tunnel down here, but figured it was just that. A rumor. Well, we have some curious minded children living here in Columbus. It seems that after Samuel Hassel, who has lived here all his life – I'm sure some of you know him - well, he started telling his great-grandson, John, about a tunnel that might be down here. Eventually Sam asked me if John and John's friend, Whitey, could check out the basement."

Chief Austin glanced over the crowd, lifted his arm and pointed to John and Whitey. "There's John and Whitey sitting back there. Say hi, boys," he instructed them.

"Hi," Whitey and John mumbled, embarrassed at the attention.

"Anyway, to make a long story short, I gave the boys a couple of flashlights and told them to go for it. I never in a million years figured they'd find anything. And, I have to admit that I was totally shocked when they found that opening. So, today, we going to find out how long it is and where it goes. I've heard that it ends under the War Memorial, but we don't know that for a fact. Roger Abbott will be able to determine exactly the direction it takes and where it ends up."

Austin looked over at Abbott, who was standing by the opening, waiting for the Chief of Police to finish up so he could enter the tunnel.

"So, without further ado," Austin said. "Whenever you're ready, Roger."

Roger Abbott gave him the thumbs up, turned and crawled into the tunnel.

Whitey, who was standing so he could see

better, grabbed John's arm. "Come on. Stand up," he said.

John hesitated for a moment, then, stood up beside his friend. He looked at the opening and saw the bottom of Roger Abbott's boots, as he disappeared into the hole. "He's gone," John said softly, and sat back down.

"If I could have your attention again, please," Chief Austin said. He waited a moment for the chatter to settle down. "We anticipate that it will be at least twenty to thirty minutes before Abbott returns. So, we'd like you all to head back upstairs, where coffee, juice, and donuts are available. Officer Gorski and I will wait down here for Abbott to return from the tunnel. As soon as we know that Abbot is okay and it's safe for you to return, Officer Gorski will come back upstairs and get you. I know you probably have a lot of questions, and you will have an opportunity to ask them at that time."

John and Whitey watched as the group of people left the room. "I'm staying here," Whitey told John.

"Me, too," John said.

The two boys settled back in their chairs and stretched out their legs, trying to get comfortable, waiting for Abbott to return.

"What's Mr. H doing this morning?" Whitey asked John. "I figured he would be here."

"He's not feeling good," John replied. "That cough came back and mom said he was running a fever this morning."

"Hope he's okay," Whitey said.

"Me, too," Austin, who had been listening,

141

chimed in. "How would you two like to join the rest of the group upstairs?"

"Nah. I'm fine here," Whitey told him.

"Besides, we don't drink coffee," John added. "I don't care for the taste."

"I tried it before," Whitey told Austin. "It didn't set too well."

Chief Austin shook his head in frustration. "Let me put it this way," he said. "You need to go upstairs. I'm not asking you; I'm telling you. I can't have you here when Abbott comes out of that hole."

"Why not?" John said. "We're not doing anything wrong, are we?"

"It's not that, John. It's for your own protection. Why do you think Roger Abbott is wearing that helmet? It's to protect him from breathing in any bad air. We don't know what might be in there and we don't want to expose you to anything dangerous."

"Oh," John uttered.

"Everyone's settled in up there," Officer Gorski declared, as she walked into the room. She glanced over at the two boys. "What are they doing here?" she asked.

"I believe they were just leaving," Austin told her. "Right, boys?"

"I guess," John said, as he stood up. He glanced down at Whitey and frowned. "Come on, Whitey. Let's go before Chief Austin drags us out of here."

Austin grinned. "Now you get the picture."

Whitey stood up and started to follow John out of the room. Movement from the opening caught his eye and he turned to see Roger Abbott coming out of the opening. He jabbed John in the back. "Wait. He's back already," he said.

Austin hurried over to Abbott and helped him out of the opening. Abbott stood up and pulled the helmet off of his head. "The tunnel doesn't end under the memorial," he blurted out.

"Well, then, where does it go," Austin asked.

"According to my calculations – which need to be confirmed, of course –it looks like it ends under the street, between the memorial and the bank. I'd say closer to the bank, though."

"I'll be damned," Austin uttered. "I never expected to hear that. So, you figure someone dug a tunnel to get into the bank's basement?"

"That could be," Abbott told him. "If that was the case, they never finished it. The thing is, though, the farther in it goes, the wider it gets. I'd say it's about five feet by five feet. It's braced up in a few places, but we already figured that was the case. There's something else, but. . ." He looked over at the two boys and hesitated. "I don't know if I should say in front of the kids."

"Forget them," Austin said, impatiently. "What else?"

"I found bones in there, Augie," he said.

"Animal bones?" Austin asked him, hoping that the answer would be positive.

"Sorry, but no," Abbott told him. "There's at least one skeleton in there. I came back out the minute I saw it. I didn't want to disturb anything. "

"Shit!" Austin muttered, under his breath.

"You need to call someone," Abbott said.

"I know," Austin said. "Officer Gorski, would you go call the coroner? If those bones are human, we need him here as soon as possible. And, tell those people upstairs that they can go home now."

"What reason should I give them?"

"Just tell that. . ." he hesitated.

"Why not tell them that the air is bad down here and you don't want them to get sick," John suggested.

Austin glanced at him and, then, looked back at Gorski. "Tell them that. . . Hell, just tell them what he said."

"Got it," Gorski said.

"Now, you two, out of here," Austin said. "There's nothing more to see."

John and Whitey slowly headed for the door. John looked at Austin and smiled. "Thanks for letting us be here today," he said.

"Just get out of here, will you? And, if it's at all possible, keep your mouths shut about what you just heard, will you? People are going to find out about this soon enough without you spreading it all over town."

"Can I tell Gramps?" John asked.

"Nobody! Understand?" Austin told him.

"Nobody, but Gramps. Right?" John said, as he ran by Austin and up the stairs.

Austin stared at Whitey, who was still standing by the doorway. "What are you waiting for?"

"Nothing," Whitey told him, and made a mad dash to the stairs.

Twenty

"You solved a murder," John shouted, as he ran into Samuel's bedroom.

Julia, who was standing by Samuel's bed, turned towards her son. "Shh," she whispered. "You'll wake him."

John looked at the old man, mouthed 'sorry' to his mother, turned around, and left the room.

Samuel opened his eyes and smiled. "I'm awake," he said. "Tell him to come back in here. I want to hear all about it."

"I don't know if that's a good idea, Grandpa. The doctor said you need your rest," Julia told him.

"I sure won't rest now, wondering what happened this morning. Please, just tell John to come back in here."

"I don't see what harm it can do," Isaac said.

Julia turned and looked at him. "I didn't know you were home," she said.

"I just got back a few minutes ago. I'd like to hear what John has to say, too."

Julia hesitated a moment. "I guess it's okay, as long as we keep it short."

"John, get in here," Isaac called out. "Grandpa's awake."

John walked into the room and went to the side of Samuel's bed. "How are you feeling?" he asked.

"I'm fine, John. But, I'll feel a lot better once you tell me what happened this morning."

"It was great," John said, grinning. "We watched that engineer guy go into the tunnel, and then Chief

Austin told all the people to go upstairs for coffee and donuts, but Whitey and me lagged behind. The guy had this funny suit on that covered his whole body and he wore a helmet over his whole head. But, the front was glass, so he could see okay. Whitey and me were just hanging around, talking to Chief Austin, when the guy came out of the tunnel. He wasn't in there very long. Anyway, he said that the tunnel didn't go to the statue. He. . ."

"You mean the war memorial?" Isaac asked.

"Yeah, that. He told Chief Austin that it was closer to the bank. But, not all the way. I mean, it went that direction but it stopped before the bank." John stopped talking and looked at Samuel, waiting for a reaction.

"Go on," Samuel said. "What about what you shouted when you came in before? About solving a murder."

"You were right about a body being in there," John told him. "The reason that guy came out of the tunnel so quick is because he found bones. Human bones, he told Chief Austin."

"Are you serious?" Julia asked, a shocked look on her face.

"I knew it," Samuel exclaimed.

"Take it easy, Grandpa," Isaac said.

"I'm fine," Samuel told him. "Was it a woman they found?" he asked John.

John looked confused for a moment. "The guy didn't say. Can you tell if it's a man or a woman by just looking at the bones?"

"Of course not," Samuel said. "That was a dumb

146

question I asked, John."

"What happened after that?" Julia asked.

"Nothing. Well, he told that lady cop to call the coroner and to send those people home. You know, the ones, who were still waiting upstairs. Then, Whitey and me left. Oh, yeah, he told us not to tell anybody, so you can't say anything."

"I'll bet you anything they find out that the body is Von Schmidt's wife, Elise," Samuel commented. "Her disappearance never did make much sense, and Von Schmidt never made much of an effort to find her."

"Well, now, Grandpa, we don't know that for sure. I guess we'll just have to wait and see," Isaac said.

"John, did the man that went into the tunnel say anyth. . ."

"His name was Abbott," John interrupted.

"You mean like in Abbott and Costello?" Julia asked.

"I guess," John replied.

"Did Abbott mention if there was only the one body in there?" Isaac asked his son.

John thought for a moment. "I think so. No, wait. I remember that he told Chief Austin that there was at least one body in there. So, there could be more, I guess."

"Well, isn't that something," Julia declared. "Now, everyone get out. Grandpa needs to rest."

Samuel laid his head back on his pillow, smiling. "You certainly had an interesting morning, John. I'm glad you were able to be there."

"Me, too," John said. "Thanks, Gramps."

"Now, we just have to wait to find out who it is," Isaac said, as he left the room.

"When do you think we'll hear something about the bones they found?"

"Never," John answered. "I think they know and they just aren't going to tell anybody. It's been almost two months already."

"I heard that a person who's called a forensic anthropologist has to do it. They sent the bones away to one of those people," Whitey told him.

"How do you know that?" John asked.

"I heard it somewhere."

"Well, you didn't tell me about it."

"I don't tell you everything, you know," Whitey said.

"Well, you should have told me that."

"I forgot," Whitey said, shrugging. "So, sue me."

"Maybe, I will and I'll forget to tell you."

Whitey looked at him, frowning. "That doesn't make any sense."

"Yeah, well, it makes sense to me."

"What are you doing over Christmas vacation?" Whitey asked John, changing topics. "Anything special?"

"Nah. Mom and dad talked about visiting my aunt who lives near Chicago, but Gramps hasn't been feeling very good, so we're gonna stay home. What about you?"

Whitey shook his head no. "We never do anything. You know that. Same crap all the time. I can't remember the last time we went on a vacation.

148

My dad never stops working. I think he'd rather work than be at home with us."

"He's just a workaholic, that's all," John said.

"I guess he might be," Whitey replied. "At least your dad takes you places."

"That's all gonna end now, with us graduating from high school and all. Are you asking anyone to the senior dance next month?

"I don't know. I was thinking about asking Penny, but I think she might already have a date," Whitey told him.

"Well, the only way you're gonna find out is to ask her," John said.

"I guess. Are you going with Sarah?"

"Yeah. Do you have to buy your date a corsage? I mean, is it like a law or something?" John asked. "I think it's just a waste of money."

"Girls like that kind of shit," Whitey said. "Just don't get an orchid. They're the most expensive ones."

"I know they are. Some people think that if it's more expensive, it must be better. That's a load of crap. Plus, they just die right away. Oh, yeah, here's a double plus. We have to buy that flower that goes on our jacket. That's even more money we have to spend on something stupid. What do they call that? A buttonair?"

Whitey laughed. "I think it's called abootinair, not a buttonair. But, I think the girl pays for it."

"Whatever," John said. "I still think it's a waste of money."

Twenty-one

Julia picked up the paper, shook the snow off of it, and hurried back into the house. "Here's your paper, Grandpa," she said, handing it to him.

Samuel took the paper from her and opened it to the front page. "Well, I'll be," he murmured, to himself.

"What?" Julia asked.

"Listen to this. 'Remains Found in Secret Tunnel Remain Unidentified," he said, reading the headlines. "Wait. It continues and says that they are most likely a woman of Negro ancestry.

"So, it wasn't Elise Von Schmidt after all," Julia said.

"I would have bet anything that it was her."

"What else does the article say?" Julia asked.

Samuel was quiet as he read through the news article. "It seems there were also some bones in there that belong to a second person." He picked up his coffee cup, and took a swallow. "I wonder who those belong to."

"Who else went missing around that time?" Julia asked him.

"I can't think of anyone. The article doesn't say how long they've been in there."

"You know, I've heard talk about an underground railroad being here. Perhaps, she was a slave who ran away."

"Anything's possible, Julia. I learned that a long time ago."

Well, I'm sure the authorities will figure it out," Julia said. She picked up the want ad section of the paper and started to browse through it. "The Corner Drug Store is looking for part time help," she told Samuel.

Samuel smiled. "Are you trying to find me a job?" he asked her.

"I'm thinking about getting a job. Something part time, maybe."

"What does Isaac think of that idea?"

"It hasn't come up and I don't think it will. Right?"

"Don't worry. I'm not going to say anything."

"Anyway, it wouldn't be until next summer, after school is out. John will probably go into the Army and I'm going to have a lot of free time on my hands," she said.

"I think it's the Navy, not the Army," Samuel corrected her.

"Really? He's decided on the Navy?"

"Last I heard," Samuel told her.

"So, you know about it already? That didn't take long. Oh, I see. So, they've been working on it all this time." Julia listened to the person on the phone for a moment. "Well, I feel bad, even it was a long time ago," Julia said.

John looked up from the program he was watching on TV, wondering what his mother felt bad about. "What?" he mouthed to his mother, who shook her head, indicating he shouldn't bother her.

"Well, that's the last thing in the world I would ever have imagined," she continued.

"What?" John asked again. Julia glanced over at

151

him, and pointed to the newspaper lying on the table next to him. John grabbed the paper, opened it to the front page, and read the headlines. "Remaining Bones in Tunnel Identified as Young Child." He read through the rest of the article, which stated the other bones were most likely those of a little girl around eight or nine years old. Further testing proved that she was definitely a daughter, or an extremely close relative, to the woman who had been found.

"Man," John uttered, as his mom hung up the phone. "This story just gets better all the time."

"I don't think it's a good story when people have died, John."

"I didn't mean it that way. It's just that it never ends. It's even a bigger mystery now. Like, how did they get in there? Were they runaway slaves? Who helped them? There are so many unanswered questions."

"We'll probably never know, John. I imagine whoever could tell us has probably died already."

"Well, Gramps is still alive. He just doesn't know anything about it. You know, Mom, I didn't really think all that stuff happened in that house. I kinda thought that Gramps was just making some of it up to make it more interesting. But, I guess it really happened."

"You know the library has a lot of old archived newspapers," Julia said. "Maybe, that would be a good project for you and Whitey this summer."

"Really, Mom? I think we have a lot of other things to do this summer besides reading old newspapers."

"Suit yourself. It was just a thought. Breakfast will be ready in a few minutes. Would you tell Grandpa to wash up, please?"

A few minutes later, John walked up to his mother, put her arms around her, and hugged her. She looked at him, wondering what he was doing and saw the tears streaming down his cheeks. She pulled away, shaking her head. "No," she cried out.

"I'm so sorry, Mom," John said. "He looked like he was sleeping. I tried to wake him, but he. . ." He turned away, unable to continue.

Julia sunk into a kitchen chair, sobbing. She looked up at John, trying to get her emotions under control. "I've got to tell your dad. Do you know where here went?"

"He went to the hardware store. He should be home soon."

Julia grabbed the hand towel and wiped her eyes. "He died in his sleep," she declared.

"It looks that way," John said.

"Thank God," she uttered softly. "I guess we better call Dr. Poszert," she told John.

"Why?" John asked her, puzzled by her comment. "Gramps is gone. He can't do anything," he declared, starting to cry again.

"I know, John. But, we still have to call him."

"Sorry about your Gramps," Whitey said, as he slid into the seat next to John.

"Thanks for coming," John whispered.

"I'm gonna miss that old fart."

"Yeah, me, too," John told him, starting to tear up.

Whitey looked around the church. "Lots of people here," he stated.

"I guess."

"At least the weather is nice," Whitey commented.

"It's too cold to bury him today," John said.

"What?" Whitey said. "Then, where do they put him?"

"In a vault, I guess. That's what I heard my dad tell someone."

Whitey glanced up at the ceiling. "Nice church," he said.

John turned and looked at him. "Did you just now notice that? You've gone to church here since you were born."

Whitey grinned. "I just wanted to see if you were paying attention."

John smiled. "Idiot."

"Are you still going to the dance next week?" Whitey asked John.

"I don't know if I should. Mom says we have to keep on living, but I'm not really in the mood."

"Shhh," whispered a woman, who was sitting in the pew behind them.

John turned and gave her a dirty look.

"What a bitch," Whitey mouthed to his friend.

John grinned.

"It's the last big dance of the year," Whitey continued. "You gotta go. It won't be any fun without you. Besides, we're doubling."

154

"I guess I'll go. I'm kinda planning on getting to third base with Sarah."

Whitey poked him in the ribs. "You dog. Is your dad gonna let you use his Packard?"

"Will you two kindly be quiet?" the woman asked. "This is funeral, for goodness sake. Show some respect, will you?"

John turned and stared at her. "My grandfather's funeral hasn't even started yet. And, there is no one in the world that I respected more than him. So, if you have a problem with us, why don't you change seats?"

"Well, I never. . ." she mumbled.

Hearing a commotion, John looked towards the back of the church and saw the priest coming down the aisle. "This is it," he told Whitey, as he stood up. "Today is the day we say good-bye to Gramps."

"Amen, to that," Whitey whispered.

The two boys remained silent as they watched the altar boys light the candles. The priest looked over the mourners and made the sign of the cross, ready to begin the funeral service.

Whitey leaned closer to John and whispered, "I forget. Which one is third base?"

Twenty-two

"I think I'm going to ask Sarah to marry me," John said.

"No way, man. You're too fucking young."

"That's your opinion. We've been going together since high school. In two years, when I get out of the Navy, I'll be twenty-two and ready to settle down."

"Not me," Whitey exclaimed. "There are way too many women out there to settle for just one."

"Remember when Gramps said you'd be married before me?" John asked.

"He sure missed that one," Whitey replied. "What's Sarah doing now? Last time you and I talked, she was working in Madison."

"She's back in town, living at home."

"Why? I thought she couldn't wait to get out of that house.

"She got a pretty nice job offer from Borden's, so she took it. Her dad doesn't charge her any rent to live at home. He just wants her to clean the house once a week. Plus, it gives her a chance to save money."

"You want another Coke?" Whitey asked.

"Sure. Make it a cherry Coke this time," John said.

"Hey, Marlene," Whitey shouted. "Bring us a large cherry Coke and a large regular Coke."

Marlene walked out from behind the counter and stared at Whitey. "Listen, you piece of crap. I don't care if you are home on leave. You don't yell in the drugstore. If you want something, you get your ass out of that booth and come and tell me. Got it?"

Whitey grinned, as he lit up a cigarette. "Whatcha gonna do if I don't? Beat me up?"

Marlene took a step closer to him. "Is that an invitation, little man? Because, I'll knock you right out of those shiny shoes of yours."

"He didn't mean anything, Marlene," John said. "Whitey, tell Marlene you're sorry.

Whitey glanced over at Marlene. "Sorry," he whispered.

"What? I can't hear you," she said.

"I'm sorry. Okay?" Whitey repeated, louder this time.

"All right, then," Marlene said, turned and walked back behind the counter. "Two cherry Cokes, it is."

"No, I want a. . ."

"Leave it alone," John said, "before she kicks the shit out of you."

The two young men walked out of the Corner Drug Store and headed towards Sarah's house. "You sure she doesn't care if I come along?" Whitey asked.

"Why would she care?" John asked.

"Well, you don't have much of your leave left and I'm sure she wants to spend as much time with you as possible."

"It's the middle of the morning. What do you think we're going to do?"

"I'd know what I'd be doing," Whitey said.

"You need a girlfriend," John said, laughing.

"What are those trucks doing there?" Whitey asked, referring to two big trucks parked on the side of

Sarah's house.

"Oh, yeah, I forgot to tell you. Sarah's dad is having that cement cistern tore out. You remember it, don't you?"

"Yeah. We saw it when we went through her house that day," Whitey recalled.

"Right. It's a hell of a job. Someone filled it in years ago. So, they have to remove all the stones and dirt and stuff first. Then, I guess, when they get all that out, they break up the cement wall and take it away."

"Isn't that gonna leave a hell of a mess?" Whitey asked.

"I think they'll clean it up and put in a new cement floor where the cistern was."

"Seems like a lot of work," Whitey muttered.

They walked up the side porch steps and looked through the screen door.

"Come on in," Sarah yelled. "I'm in the kitchen."

"How'd she know we were here?" Whitey asked.

"She's a witch. She senses these things," John told him, grinning.

"Don't call me a witch," Sarah said, as John gave her a kiss on the cheek.

"Is it okay if I go downstairs and watch them?" Whitey asked her.

"Go ahead. You know where the basement is." She picked up a towel and started drying her hands. "How did you two manage to get leave at the same time?" Sarah asked, as Whitey slammed the basement door shut. "He's like a bull in a china shop," she added.

158

"He's okay," John told her. "I've never seen him accidently break anything."

"Just on purpose," Sarah said, smiling.

"How long are those guys gonna be working down there?" John asked her.

"I have no idea, but I can't wait for them to finish it. They are just about done clearing the debris out of it, but, after that, they have to take down that cement wall."

"Why'd your dad decide to do it now, anyway? It wasn't hurting anything."

"I think it's a health thing. He heard something about mold build up and I guess mold is bad for you. I can't believe all the stuff they've found in there," Sarah said.

"Like what?"

The basement door flew open, banging against the wall.

Sarah turned to see Whitey standing in the doorway. "Really, Whitey, can't you be more careful. I don't want to have to explain to my dad how a hole got in the wall."

"Sorry," Whitey said. "Poop, you gotta get down here and take a look at all the junk they're are finding in that cistern thing."

Sarah smiled. "I guess it's easier for you to go look than for me to tell you."

John headed towards the basement door. "Aren't you coming," he asked when Sarah didn't follow him.

"No. You go ahead. I don't like it down there."

"I'm tired of it," she told Wilbur. "You bring these

159

people into our house and expect me to wait on them hand and foot. Things need to change. I'm not your slave and I need help."

"And, just how do you expect to pay for this help you demand? I'm not spending my hard earned money on such foolishness."

She looked at him and laughed. "Your hard earned money? You haven't worked hard a day in your life. Either you get me help, or so help me god, I'll take the children and leave you."

"And, where will you go?"

"Anywhere away from you and your lover boy," she shouted.

She knew she had gone too far, as she watched him take off his belt. "Get upstairs," he yelled at her.

"No!"

"Now," he shouted, as he grabbed her arm and twisted it. "We're going to have ourselves a little party."

"Please, no. I'm sorry. I'm just tired, that's all."

"Get up those stairs," he demanded, as he started pushing her.

She suddenly turned and shoved him away from her, and made a dash for the door. Wilbur fell backwards, landing hard on his butt. Just as she reached for the handle, the door swung open. She was staring into the face of Albert Borden.

"Grab her," Wilbur yelled.

Borden pushed her back into the room, grinning. "Are you being a bad girl again, Elise?" he asked.

"Don't you touch me," she yelled.

Wilbur walked up behind her and grabbed her by her hair. "Come along, darling, I think we'll take this

160

little party to the basement. Are you coming, Albert?"

"I wouldn't miss it for the world," he replied, following them into the kitchen.

"Wait. Would you do me a favor first?" Wilbur asked him.

"Of course. What is it?"

"Would you mind getting a couple shovels out of the garage? We have some digging to do."

"Sarah," John shouted.

Sarah glanced at the clock, surprised that almost half an hour had gone by since Whitey and John had gone down to the basement.

"Sarah," John yelled again.

She opened the basement door and looked down the steps. "What do you want?" she called.

"Call Chief Austin and tell him to get over here," John said, as he came to the bottom of the stairs and looked up at her.

"What should I tell him?"

"Tell him that one of men working here just pulled some bones out of the cistern. And, they look human, Sarah. I'm pretty sure they just found Elise Von Schmidt."

Sarah stared at John. "You're kidding, right?"

"He's not kidding," Whitey yelled. "Tell Austin I told them to stop digging. What we have now, lady and gentlemen, is a crime scene."

"That's not funny, Whitey," Sarah shouted. "I need to call my dad."

"Call Austin first," John instructed. He waited until he saw her go back into the kitchen, then, turned

161

to Whitey. "I'd give anything if Gramps was here. He knew that Von Schmidt woman would be found here or in that tunnel. He was right, Whitey. He was right all the time."

"Yeah, but he really thought it was the tunnel," Whitey said. "Remember, they filled in the cistern when she was still living here."

"They only used dirt and some small stones. It would have been easy enough to dig a hole and bury her in there," John responded.

She shook the dirt off of her body and yawned. It had been years since she had seen daylight. She mostly wandered the halls during the night, checking on the family that occupied the bedrooms. Of all the families that had occupied her home throughout the years, she liked this family the best. She wasn't sure, when they first moved in, if she was going to allow them to stay. But, once that horrible woman left, she found it rather pleasant to have them living here. She looked around the room and smiled. Everything was good now. It was time to go.

"What the hell?" Whitey said, flinching. He turned and looked behind him. "Did you feel that?" Whitey whispered. "I just felt a rush of cold air. It felt like it passed right through me. Geez, it gave me the shivers."

"What the hell is that smell?" one of the workmen yelled. "My god, that's foul. I need some fresh air. Let's get out of here," he shouted, as he started to cough.

The three men, who had been working to remove the cistern, turned and ran out the trapdoor to the outside.

John and Whitey stood at the bottom of the stairs, not moving. "Do you smell anything?" John asked.

"I don't know. It smells musty, but I'm not sure what they smelled." Whitey sniffed the air and made a face. "Now I smell it. It smells a lot like rotten eggs," he said. "Did you fart?" he asked John, grinning.

"No, I didn't fart."

"Oh, that is gross," Whitey suddenly said, holding his nose.

"I'm out of here," John said, as the stench got stronger.

Whitey didn't move.

"Are you coming?" John asked him, as he started up the stairs.

"I can't."

"What do you mean, you can't?"

"Something is touching me on my shoulder. I don't want to move. Do you see it?"

John turned and walked back down the stairs. He looked Whitey over and grinned.

"It's a piece of rope hanging from the ceiling. You must have brushed against it. Boy, are you a baby. And, you call yourself an Army man," he said, laughing.

"Hey, the smell is gone," Whitey said. "I wonder what it was."

Sarah smiled as they walked into the kitchen. "I

was nervous for you," she told John. "What happened down there? I heard yelling and now those guys are all in the back yard."

"There was a horrible smell. Like really bad," John told her.

"It smelled like rotten eggs," Whitey informed her. "Could you smell it up here?"

"I didn't smell anything," Sarah told him.

John turned as Chief Austin walked into the kitchen, shaking his head.

'I should have known Trouble and More Trouble would be here. What's all this about bones being found?" he asked.

"It just might be the missing Von Schmidt woman," John told him.

"You think so?" Austin inquired.

Whitey grinned. "Who else would it be? And, I don't think Mrs. Von Schmidt was very happy about being dug up."

Austin looked at him, a little confused by his comment. "And, just why would that be?"

"Well, she sure made a big stink about it," he told Austin, laughing.

Epilogue

John looked down at the young boy, who was playing on the floor, and smiled. Never in a million years did he think that such a tiny creature could bring him so much joy. He had loved raising his children, but this little boy – his first grandson - made his heart swell every time he saw him.

"Grandpa, tell me a story," Harry said, as he climbed onto his lap.

"Which book do you want me to read to you?

"No, Grandpa. Tell me one of your stories. I like your stories best."

"How about I tell you about my great-grandfather? His name was Samuel and he used to tell me the best stories ever."

"Okay. I like stories about him."

"Samuel was a really nice man and he was really old when he died."

"How old?"

"He was ninety years old and. . ."

"That's really old," Harry interrupted. "Are you ninety years old?"

John smiled. "Not yet." He adjusted the little boy on his lap. "Are you comfortable?"

Harry snuggled up against him and sighed.

"When I was still in school, my friend and I used to listen to my Gramps tell us stories about different things that happened here in this town."

"What was your friend's name?"

"Whitey. His name was Whitey and we had some of the best adventures together."

"Where's Whitey now?"

"Whitey went to heaven. He's with Gramps now."

"Do you miss him?"

"Every day. I miss him every day. You would have liked him, Harry. He was so funny.

"Did he make you laugh?"

"All the time. Anyway, Gramps told us about a tunnel that ran under a street by City Hall and Whitey and I wanted to see it. So, one day a nice policeman let us go down in the basement of City Hall and look around. And, guess what?"

"What?" Harry asked.

"There really was a tunnel down there."

"Did you go in it?" Harry asked, his eyes slowly starting to close.

"No. but we saw the man who did."

"Can I go see it?" Harry asked.

"It's not there anymore. Some men came and filled it all in. But, there is something else I can show you. It's a great big theater and, when you get bigger, we'll go there some day. One time, Whitey and I climbed up the fire escape and went in through an open window. We almost got caught, but we. . ."

John looked down at the sleeping child, and smiled. And, someday, when you're older, he thought, I'll tell you all about the house on Ludington Street.

Author's Remarks, Notes, and Clarifications.

It's interesting how a story can come to life. Sometimes, it's nothing more than a remark made in passing, or finding out, sixty years after the fact, that someone you used to know was called Poop by his best friend.

I was surprised to learn that it wasn't illegal to drink alcohol during prohibition. The 18th Amendment only forbade the "manufacture, sale and transportation of intoxicating liquors" – not their consumption. By law, any wine, beer, or spirits Americans had stashed away in January, 1920 were theirs to keep and enjoy in the privacy of their homes. For most, this amounted to only a few bottles, but some affluent drinkers built cavernous wine cellars and even bought out whole liquor store inventories to ensure they had healthy stockpiles of legal hooch.

The worlds' largest litter of domestic cats were born on August 7, 1970, when a Burmese/Siamese cat belonging to V. Gane of Kingham, Oxfordshire, UK, gave birth to 19 kittens, four of which were stillborn.

When I was growing up, we always said breakfast, dinner, and supper, not breakfast, lunch, and dinner. I don't know when it changed, but when I say dinner in this book, it means what we now call lunch.

Research is important to me when I write, as I try to get the facts as accurate as possible. While writing this book, I learned that a male swan is called a cob, the female is known as a pen, and the babies are called cygnets.

Lastly, for those of you are still confused, here are the four bases. They can vary, but basically this is the popular consensus:

First base = kissing, including open-mouth (or French) kissing.

Second base = petting above the waist, including touching, feeling, and fondling the chest and breasts,

Third base = petting or orally stimulating below the waist, including touching, feeling, and fondling all the good places

Home base = sexual intercourse

About the Author

For updates and information regarding Susan and her novels, please visit www.susanlpare.com.

Made in the USA
Columbia, SC
22 October 2018